Escape to beautiful Tuscany and Lake Como in this romantic new duet

One Summer in Italy

From Harlequin Romance author
Michelle Douglas

Frankie Weaver and Audrey Dimarco are cousins in Australia—and when their late grandmother leaves them a bequest to spend the summer in Italy, they can't wait to start their travels!

Frankie has big decisions to make about her future, while Audrey has new family members to meet near Lake Como...but both find their Italian escapades result in romantic encounters that could change all their plans!

Book 1: *Unbuttoning the Tuscan Tycoon*

On sale February 2023

Book 2: *Cinderella's Secret Fling*

On sale June 2023

Dear Reader,

I think most of us have had a fantasy of running away from our daily grind and heading somewhere fabulous to indulge in some serious R & R. On one particularly fraught afternoon, I wondered what it'd be like to have a whole summer away. That's how the One Summer in Italy duet was born.

In *Unbuttoning the Tuscan Tycoon*, my burned-out heroine Frankie gets to spend the summer on a beautiful vineyard in the rolling golden hills of Tuscany. She needs to make some hard decisions about her life, and she's convinced a slower pace under a warm Tuscan sun will revitalize her. This summer, she's determined to be carefree and laid-back. Her new boss, Dante, though, has other plans for her—and he's as buttoned-up as they come!

As these two opposites butt heads, negotiate, agree and disagree, they find themselves more and more drawn to each other. But he's a workaholic while she's trying to be a free spirit. Can one magical summer lead to true love? Frankie and Dante's story was a joy to write—a true escape—and I hope you enjoy their adventures, not to mention the sigh-worthy setting, as much as I did.

Hugs,

Michelle

Unbuttoning the Tuscan Tycoon

Michelle Douglas

Recycling programs
for this product may
not exist in your area.

ISBN-13: 978-1-335-73701-4

Unbuttoning the Tuscan Tycoon

Harlequin Enterprises ULC
22 Adelaide St. West, 41st Floor
Toronto, Ontario M5H 4E3, Canada
www.Harlequin.com

Printed in U.S.A.

Michelle Douglas has been writing for Harlequin since 2007 and believes she has the best job in the world. She lives in a leafy suburb of Newcastle, on Australia's east coast, with her own romantic hero, a house full of dust and books, and an eclectic collection of '60s and '70s vinyl. She loves to hear from readers and can be contacted via her website, michelle-douglas.com.

Books by Michelle Douglas

Harlequin Romance

Miss Prim's Greek Island Fling
The Maid, the Millionaire and the Baby
Redemption of the Maverick Millionaire
Singapore Fling with the Millionaire
Secret Billionaire on Her Doorstep
Billionaire's Road Trip to Forever
Cinderella and the Brooding Billionaire
Escape with Her Greek Tycoon
Wedding Date in Malaysia
Reclusive Millionaire's Mistletoe Miracle

Visit the Author Profile page
at Harlequin.com for more titles.

With thanks and gratitude to the Hunter Writers
Centre, City of Newcastle and the Port Authority
of New South Wales for creating the Nobbys-
Whibayganba Lighthouse Arts residency program.
These studio spaces are such a boon to local
creatives and visitors alike. It has been an honor to
take part in the program.

Praise for
Michelle Douglas

PROLOGUE

FRANKIE GLANCED ACROSS the table at Audrey. Nonna's restaurant was hushed in a way it never had been before, the shades at the windows drawn and the door firmly shut. Audrey looked as glum and gutted as she felt. She lit the table's candle, but it did little to dispel the gloom.

She hadn't thought she had any tears left, but her vision blurred. Audrey instantly reached across and covered Frankie's hand. She managed to send her cousin a watery smile. 'I miss her so much.'

After today's reading of the will, the fact they'd never see their beloved nonna again had become all too real.

Audrey's grip tightened, and her chin wobbled. If Audrey started crying, Frankie would start howling and—

'We promised her we'd be strong,' she croaked.

Both women straightened, pushed their shoulders back.

Audrey gestured around. 'I expect they'll sell it.'

Frankie tried to keep her voice level. 'It's no doubt the sensible thing to do.'

The will had held no surprises. Nonna's children—Audrey's father and Frankie's mother—had inherited equal shares of Nonna's estate, with both Audrey and Frankie receiving...

Frankie glanced at the A4 envelopes on the table in front of them. One of them Audrey's, the other hers. Nonna had left them whatever was in those envelopes.

Neither she nor Audrey had been in any hurry to open them. Audrey gestured. 'Once I open it... It's just... It all seems so final.'

Audrey had the kindest heart on the planet. And the softest. Frankie needed to be strong for her. She needed to be strong for them both.

'She loved us both so much.' Reaching out, she gripped both of Audrey's hands. 'And she'll live on in our hearts forever. One day when we have children, we'll regale them with stories about Nonna and her restaurant, and they'll come to love her too.' For a moment that vision filled her soul.

Audrey's mouth curved into the smile that never failed to lighten Frankie's heart. 'We will.' Pulling in a breath, she nodded. 'It's time.'

With a final squeeze, they released each other's hands and reached for their envelopes.

Frankie pulled forth a letter. With trembling hands, she unfolded it.

My darling Frankie,
You know how much I love you. What you may not realise is how much I worry for you.

She blinked.

Do not become a slave to duty. Do not become a slave to others' expectations. If I had one wish for you, my darling girl, it would be that you have the opportunity to forge your own path—one that will bring you happiness and satisfaction. Life is so much more than work. Do not forget to live, and love, and find joy in your life.

The words speared into the sorest part of her heart.

Frankie, you need a holiday. You need the time to evaluate your life and weigh up all your options.

She didn't have time for a holiday! She didn't…

Will you please do your nonna one final favour and make my wish for you come true? I ask that you spend this summer in Tuscany. You always spoke about doing so as a teenager—your eyes lighting up as you told me in the greatest detail how you planned to work and tour the area, enjoying the sights and the sounds…and the freedom, as you found out about your family who had once come from there.

The sudden memory of those old dreams burned through her. Once they'd made her ache with anticipation and tremble with excitement.

Her heart started to pound. Maybe Nonna was right. Maybe it was time for Frankie to pull her head from the sand and face a few hard facts, make some hard decisions. She swallowed. Decisions that would have a lasting impact on her life.

You stopped talking about it after your father died. Frankie, my dearest girl, you need to start dreaming again. Please, will you do this one thing for me?

Tears blurred her vision. Blinking hard, she returned to the envelope to discover an air ticket to Rome, a modest cheque to cover travelling expenses and a small velvet box. Lifting the lid, she found a silver pendant of a bird in flight—a symbol of freedom. She immediately fastened it about her throat.

When she glanced across at Audrey, she found her cousin staring at an air ticket of her own. Frankie cleared her throat. 'I'm off to Tuscany. You?'

'Lake Como. Wide eyes lifted to hers. 'When are you planning to leave?'

The European summer had already started, but… 'In two weeks.'

Audrey gulped. 'Make it one week and we could travel as far as Rome together.'

She didn't give herself time to think or waver. 'Deal.'

They shook on it.

CHAPTER ONE

FRANKIE PULLED BERTHA, her sky-blue Kombi van, onto the hard shoulder and surveyed the huge wooden sign above a rather imposing set of gates. They were a tasteful combination of stone and wood, giving them an impression of permanence and prosperity. Of wealth.

They were the kind of gates that knew their purpose.

Unlike you.

She wrinkled her nose, tried to blow a raspberry at the needling voice full of censure.

You should be settling on your medical specialty, not gallivanting.

'I'm not gallivanting!'

Three months, that was all she was asking. *Three months.*

On cue, her phone rang. Staring at the name on the screen, she was tempted to ignore it. Guilt got the better of her and at the last moment she pressed it to her ear. 'Mum.'

'Frankie, you know how worried I am about you and—'

'Hi, I'm great! How are you?'

There was a pause at the other end.

'Sorry, Mum, terrible timing. I'll have to call you back.'

Dropping the phone to the seat beside her, she blinked hard. Why couldn't her mother just be happy for her? Why couldn't she tell her to have a lovely holiday? Why—

A fist tightened about her chest squeezing the air from her lungs. Closing her eyes, she concentrated on her breathing.

You have a whole summer in Tuscany.

She didn't need to choose her medical specialty yet. She didn't need to know if medicine was her future. She didn't need to know *anything*.

Opening her eyes, she straightened. She had time. Nonna had made sure of it. And she had no intention of wasting the gift her grandmother had given her. She'd focus on the here and now.

And the here and now were those gates and that sign.

The sign read Vigna di Riposo—Vineyard of Rest—with carved grapevines bracketing the words. Brass plaques on the gates were etched with fat bunches of grapes. It might look fancy, but an unpretentious warmth threaded through it too.

'Right.' She clapped her hands. 'We're going to be chilled and laid-back.' Two words that were completely alien to her, but ones she meant to master over the course of the summer.

Carefree and happy-go-lucky, that was her catchphrase. She was in Tuscany, the beautiful heartland of Italy, and this was dream-come-true stuff. She *would* relax.

Deep inside, a flicker of excitement began to burn. For the next six weeks she'd be based here at this beautiful vineyard. She'd arrived several weeks before the grapes were due to be harvested, but Senor Silva had said that he would find jobs for her to do prior to the picking—odd jobs like preparing the staff quarters for the mass arrival of the seasonal staff. It all sounded gloriously mindless.

She did a happy dance in her seat. She didn't have any other responsibilities, wasn't in charge of making any momentous decisions that would impact other people's lives, wouldn't need to make any split-second decisions that could have life and death consequences. *Perfection!*

In her mind's eye, she saw herself as a puffy dandelion seed head and the image made her feel light and free. All of Tuscany was her playground for the next three months. She *would* make the most of it.

Driving through the gates, she pointed Bertha up the gravelled drive. Topping the rise, her jaw dropped at the vista that spread before her. The view looked as if it'd been pulled from the pages of a guidebook.

In the hollow below sat a low-slung building, built of the local honey-coloured stone and accented with the same dark wood as the gates. It would be the main public building where the wine was sold and tastings took place. In the blinding summer sun, its shady interior promised ease and comfort.

Outbuildings stretched off further to her left, but it was the surrounding countryside that held her spellbound. Spreading down the hillside in front of her and along the valley, and up the slope beyond, grapevines marched in lush greenness beneath a perfect blue sky—green and gold throbbed in the air, and things inside of her that had been knotted too tight, began to loosen.

It was a classic Tuscan landscape—beautifully serene—and a sigh that seemed to last forever eased from her lungs.

Pulling Bertha into the visitors' car park, she gazed her fill, but didn't switch off the engine. This car park wasn't for employees. Signor Silva had told her to follow the road around to where she'd find the staff car park, and the seasonal quarters beyond where she'd be able to set up camp in Bertha.

She snapped a picture to send to Audrey before pushing the van into reverse. At the same moment, a man emerged from the shady interior of the building, and made a beeline for her.

The precision of his movements, and the alarming amount of ground those long legs covered, had her blinking. But any alarm she might have felt at having perhaps stepped out of line by stopping to admire the area was quickly overridden by a shock of feminine appreciation.

She swallowed, hard, her throat becoming strangely dry. She and Audrey had joked that Italian men were devastatingly handsome, but she hadn't expected to be confronted by the most beautiful man she'd ever seen on the first day of arriving at her new job.

Part-time job.

The reminder of just how much free time was now hers had her lifting her face to the sun and drawing in a breath of fragrant summer air as she waited for the man to reach her.

Raven-dark hair gleamed rich in the early afternoon sun and dark eyes that looked black from this distance connected with hers, sending a crackle of something through her, like an electrical pulse. He looked oddly familiar as if she'd seen him somewhere before. Was he a film star or some kind of celebrity?

At just over six feet, there wasn't an ounce of spare flesh on that lean muscular body. Powerful shoulders tapered to lean hips and long, strong thighs. Maybe he was an athlete? Or a dancer?

Her knowledge of either was meagre, though, so it didn't help her identify him. What she did know, was that he moved with an innate grace that had a sigh welling in her chest.

Pick your jaw up off the floor, Frankie.

She managed it just before he reached her door. 'We've been expecting you.'

He spoke perfect English in a thick—and divine—Italian accent, and—

One look at his face told her he wasn't happy about something. She straightened. 'Signor Silva? I'm very excited to be here. I hope I've not stepped on any toes by stopping to admire all of this. It's beautiful. I'll head around to the staff car park now.'

'I will show you the way.'

He strode around the van and leaped into the passenger seat. His scent—all lemon and sage and sunshine—invaded Bertha's interior, pulling oxygen out of Frankie's lungs and replacing it with something that made her head feel light. He pointed the way and, swallowing, she turned Betha in that direction, unable to utter a single sensible syllable. If forced to talk, her words would probably emerge in a gabble of *g* and *b* sounds.

Which wasn't the impression she wanted to make.

Except we're not worrying about any of that at the moment, are we?

That was right! And it wasn't like she wanted to impress the man or anything. His beauty had taken her off guard, that's all. And nobody wanted to look or sound like a fool. Her included. Even with a catchphrase of carefree and happy-go-lucky.

'Not Signor Silva,' he said now in that beautiful accent.

Signor Silva was the vineyard's staff supervisor. He'd said he'd meet her on arrival. She glanced at the man beside her, moistened her lips and swallowed carefully, doing all she could to ensure her voice would work without disgracing her. 'Then… who are you?'

'My name is Dante Alberici.'

Dante…? Summoning the research she'd done on Riposo, she sifted through her mind. Alberici…? 'Oh, my God!' She swung to him. 'You *own* Vigna di Riposo.' And a large portion of real estate in Tuscany too—including prime sites in Florence. The Alberici Corporation was world-renowned, and Dante Alberici a self-made man. 'You're the *big* boss!'

Careful of incoherent g *and* b *sounds.*

'Please do not run into that wine barrel with your van.'

She reefed her gaze back to the front and negotiated the entrance to a car park demarcated on either side with wine barrels. As the car park was hidden behind several outbuildings, it was clearly meant for staff like her.

'They might only be for decorative purposes, but I should like them to remain in one piece, yes? And your van too.'

'Yes, absolutely. That's definitely what we want. No minor prangs happening here or anything of the sort. No indeedy.'

Shut up, Frankie.

Wincing, she concentrated on parking neatly *and* safely. She and Bertha were still getting used to each other and she had no intention of disgracing herself in front of this impossibly perfect man.

'You are surprised to see me.'

It was a statement, not a question, but she figured he still expected an answer. 'I thought you'd delegate staff to a manager or supervisor.'

'Ah, but this project is one that is very dear to my heart. I wish to be involved in all of its aspects.'

Okay. So the harvest meant a lot to him. She switched off Bertha's engine. Was he in the process of making a new wine or—?

Yours is not to reason why.

That was right! Carefree and happy-go-lucky, that was her. She sent him her widest smile. 'That's very admirable.'

'Not admirable, necessary.' He didn't smile back. 'Now come with me.'

Giving her no time to reply, he was out of Ber-

tha and striding towards a side entrance of the
main building before she'd even pushed open her
door. She had to run to catch up with him.

'There is not much time for you to survey the
equipment and give us a list of anything addi-
tional you might need, but I do have suppliers on
standby.'

Equipment? For the harvest? Surely all she
needed was a bucket and gloves. And probably
some secateurs or sharp scissors or something.
And bug spray. And sunscreen. And as she'd
bought those last two with her...

She glanced at him. Noted the way his lips
pressed together, the tension in his jaw and shoulders. He was cross. With *her*. And trying not to
show it. What on earth had she done to disturb
his peace of mind?

Lifting her chin, she loosened hands that had
started to clench. She had no intention of letting
him disturb her peace. She was going to be Zen.
Very Zen.

But she wasn't Zen enough to contain a gasp
when he led her around a corner and she found
herself at the back of the main complex in an
amazing dining area. She pulled to a halt. 'That
view!'

From floor-to-ceiling windows, the undulating
valley of lush gold greenness spread before her.
The neat rows of grapevines were prolific, rich
and somehow soothing. In the middle distance a

river sparkled silver, and a line of cypresses stood tall and proud. The sky was a deep true blue with a few well-placed fluffy clouds to highlight the depth of all that blue and green.

Clasping her hands beneath her chin, she moved to the windows until her nose almost touched the glass. *In a few weeks' time she'd be on one of those hillsides, picking grapes...part of that landscape. Oh, Nonna, what an adventure.*

'You approve, yes?'

'Approve? Signor Alberici, it's *sublime.*'

'You may call me Dante.'

He stared at the view too, and for a brief moment those broad shoulders unhitched. 'It is a very pleasing picture for the eye. I think our diners will be most pleased.'

She pointed. 'The terrace is going to be *the* place to be.'

Tables sat on honey-coloured pavers, and above them a lush green vine wound around a wooden pergola. And spread before them was that view. Dante folded his arms and smiled. Her breath did a funny little one-two in her chest. Talk about a pleasing picture for the eye! He should smile more—a whole lot more.

'Your words are music to my ears.' He clapped his hands and made an abrupt about turn. 'Come with me to survey your domain.'

She pointed back towards the grapevines. Weren't *they* her domain? But he was already striding away, and she had to trot to catch up with him. Perhaps the odd-jobbing started *right now*.

He pushed through a set of swinging doors and then gestured with a flourish. 'No expense has been spared. I am hoping you will work much magic here and give my restaurant a reputation to be proud of.'

Her shoulders inched up towards her ears. Who exactly did he think she was? 'Um… Dante…' Actually, on second thoughts, she doubted he'd invite a lowly grape picker to call him by his first name. 'Signor Alberici, I think there's been some mistake. I—'

That gaze snapped back to hers, dark brows lowering over flashing eyes crackling with tension, and carefree and happy-go-lucky fled. 'We created this kitchen to *your* specifications!' He stabbed a finger in the air. 'What is wrong with it? What fault do you find?'

She held her hands up—conciliatory and mollifying. It had sometimes worked on frantic patients at the hospital. 'The kitchen is absolute perfection. The thing is—'

'We have a problem, Dante!' The kitchen doors swung open as a man with an American accent came tearing through them. 'Eleanora Toussaint has done a bunk. She's just accepted a position with a Michelin-starred restaurant in Tokyo. She flies out there this afternoon.'

'No, she's here! She—'

He swung back to Frankie, who grimaced and shrugged an apology. With a face as dark as the devil's, he swung back to the other man. 'Ring her *now* and tell her I will sue her if she does not show up as arranged.'

'I *could* do that.'

Up close she could see the other man was probably a decade older than Dante.

'Except, as she never actually *signed* the contract, a fact she just pointed out to me, I'm afraid it would be something of an empty threat.'

'Why did you not make sure it was signed!'

'Because you told me you wanted to take care of it *personally* yourself.'

A flurry of rapid-fire Italian left Dante's perfect lips—oaths and curses directed at both himself and Eleanora. He stomped around the kitchen island, waving his arms above his head, as if he couldn't contain his outrage and frustration.

The older man's eyes widened, and Frankie swallowed. She *really* didn't belong here. Time to tiptoe out, find Signor Silva, get her work instructions, and then get her carefree and happy-go-lucky vibe back on. Hopefully they could all just pretend this misunderstanding had never happened and—

She started edging towards the door, but froze when dark eyes fixed on her. 'Who in the blazes are *you*?'

His English was utter perfection when he was

in a temper—clearly enunciated and delivered with precision. She managed a weak smile and held out a hand. 'Hi, I'm Frankie Weaver. I'm here to pick grapes.'

He gave her hand a cursory shake, as if the politeness had been bred into him. But the fact that he resented having to be civil was as clear as his English. His brows drew down low over his eyes. 'Why did you not say anything? Why did you not correct my misapprehension?'

The implicit accusation put steel in her spine. 'Because I didn't initially realise you were working under a misapprehension. I only realised it once you showed me the kitchen. I was trying to tell you when Mr...' she gestured towards the other man, 'broke the clearly unwelcome news that the person you thought I was has left you in the lurch.'

Another round of rapid-fire Italian followed—mostly curses. Creative ones too, which in normal circumstances might have made her laugh. But she didn't dare laugh. She—

Why not? *She* hadn't done anything wrong. *Carefree and happy-go-lucky.* When he paused for breath, she said in perfect Italian, 'She indeed sounds like pond scum—some prehistoric slug-like creature that has dragged its sorry butt from the slime and brings with it a prehistoric stench at odds with grapevines and summer. You definitely don't want someone like that in charge of your kitchen.'

He stiffened. 'Are you mocking me, Ms Weaver?'

Oops. Okay, so maybe she hadn't got the tone quite right. She backtracked as fast as she could. 'Nope, absolutely not.'

'You speak Italian?' he snapped out.

'Si.'

Elegant nostrils flared. 'I apologise if any of the things I just said were offensive to your ears.'

He dragged a hand through short, thick hair. It was the kind of hair that looked as if it never dared be out of place. It also looked ridiculously soft and—

'I'm Michael Alcott, Dante's personal assistant.'

The other man leaned across, breaking her train of thought. *Mercifully.* She shook the outstretched hand. 'Nice to meet you.'

Michael turned back to Dante. 'I have Donna and Alessio looking for replacements, but it's not going to be possible to acquire a big name by Saturday. We might need to delay the opening.'

Dante snapped up to his full height. 'I refuse to allow that woman to derail my plans. If we delay now, Lorenzo's reputation will be tainted. People will think we are inefficient and unorganised. I refuse to allow such a thing.'

'In that case, Dante, you need to reconsider your decision and take over the chef's role. You have the skills and training.'

Those arms started waving about his head again. 'I need to be front of house! I need to be Lorenzo's eyes and ears, to ensure everything runs smoothly.' He swung to Frankie. 'Tell me you are a chef.'

'I'd…uh…love to—' *liar* '—but I'm lucky to not burn toast.' She shrugged—carefully, she didn't want him misconstruing it as her laughing at him again. 'But if *you* can cook, then you can train anyone to be a halfway decent maître d' before Saturday.'

Halfway decent…

Dante's mouth opened and closed, his hands clenching.

Halfway decent wasn't anywhere *near* good enough. Lorenzo's had to be the best.

His throat thickened. To his eternal regret, he'd not spent as much time at the vineyard during the last three or four summers as he should've. Oh, he knew Lorenzo had been proud of him, proud of all he'd achieved, but he'd also forever been telling Dante he needed to stop and smell the roses too.

His hands clenched. He should've spent more time with his grandfather during these last few years. Now he couldn't and—

Dragging in a breath, he fought for control. What he could do was take one entire summer off from running his business empire, to create a restaurant that would pay worthy tribute to the man who'd made such a difference to his life. It would be his attempt to spend one last summer with his grandfather.

This summer he'd create the restaurant of Lorenzo's dreams. He'd do everything in his power to provide the restaurant with a rock-solid foundation that they could build on. One that would not only ensure its success but set it on the path to become a leading light in culinary circles. His grandfather's name would be celebrated across the land.

Halfway decent? No. *Halfway decent* wasn't anywhere near good enough.

'Look, it's a cinch,' the woman said—what was her name again? Frankie? She strode out into the dining room and, passing by the maître d' stand, mimed picking up two menus. In rather lovely Italian—perfectly understandable, but with an accent he couldn't for the moment place—she said, 'Mr and Mrs Conti, how lovely to see you. Welcome to Lorenzo's.'

The welcome of her smile had him blinking and, in that moment, he could see why he'd mistaken her for Eleanora Toussaint. Beneath the surface warmth, Frankie had an easy and innate air of command. Like—

He clenched up so hard he started to shake. Like a chef!

Damn Eleanora Toussaint! She might not have signed a physical contract, but she'd verbally agreed to their arrangement. He could still sue her. He might not win, but he had the kind of money to drag out a suit that would tarnish her reputation.

He rubbed a hand over his face. Except he didn't want that kind of publicity for Lorenzo's. Besides, he wasn't a vindictive man. Throwing good money away on an exercise like that was utter foolishness.

He'd allowed emotion to sway him too much already. If this had been any of his other projects, he'd have done everything by the book. Instead, he'd unwisely thrown the rulebook out of the window, so delighted to have captured the attention of such a celebrated chef. He'd congratulated himself prematurely, ignoring the fact she'd delayed signing the contract.

One should not give in to emotion. He'd learned that lesson the hard way. When one allowed emotion to rule them, they risked losing everything. Like his mother had lost everything when his father had left. If she'd been able to view her husband with a clear eye, she might've protected herself from hardship, heartbreak and deprivation. He would not let that happen again—not to him, not to her, not to his sisters. And he would not let it happen to Lorenzo's now either.

'Your table is this way.'

He snapped back, his temples pounding, as Frankie led her hypothetical diners to a table by the window and seated them. Her smile held welcome while her manner exuded poise and confidence. There was something else too, but it eluded him, defying definition.

Whatever it was, it would have customers blooming beneath it like grapes under a warm Tuscan sun.

Although he'd mistaken her for Eleanora, and although he'd been vexed with her late arrival, he'd been relieved when he'd finally come face-to-face with her. Or thought he had. It was odd, but something about Frankie put him at his ease. He felt that he could depend on her.

He frowned. It would be foolishness to trust such an impression. In his experience, that immediate impression of reliability was the province of con men and those with hidden agendas. Except he had an excellent nose for those, and nothing about Frankie rang any alarm bells.

His stomach knotted as he again tried to identify the elusive quality she possessed. Maybe it wasn't a quality but the way she looked. She had an interesting face, attractive rather than beautiful, but it was a face he suspected he could stare at for a very long time without ever tiring of.

He jerked back. *Cavolo.* This woman was an employee. He did not have dalliances with employees. If the elusive quality he was trying to identify was attraction, then he would annihilate it immediately.

As if sensing the weight of his gaze, she glanced

up, and he immediately smoothed his face out. She didn't deserve his frustration. The situation he now found himself in was not of her making. However, her suggestion he find another maître d' was not one which interested him. He opened his mouth to tell her where to report to Signor Silva, when she kicked back into action.

'Yes, the seats on the terrace are the best seats in the house on an evening like this, but they're always snapped up well in advance. However, I could get you a reservation out there for a fortnight's time.' She leaned in close to her imaginary couple as if to keep her next words just between them. 'We had a cancellation not five minutes ago.'

He bit back a smile. Clever. Crafty. Yet still charming.

'Why don't you let me know if you're interested when you're leaving. I'll keep it free until then. In the meantime, this table is also among our best and I think you'll agree the view from the window is splendid. The food, I promise, will not disappoint.'

An attractive offer made without any pressure. He couldn't have done better himself. She was charm personified.

She then proceeded to rattle off a hypothetical list of the chef's specials for the evening without a single stutter or hesitation.

Beside him, Michael murmured, 'She's good.'

Then his phone rang. 'I need to take this. I'll be in my office if you need me.'

Dante nodded, his attention trained on Frankie, his mind racing. He did have the necessary skills to cook the kind of meals he dreamed of for this restaurant. It would work as a temporary measure until he could find a suitable replacement for Eleanora. It would buy him the time to woo someone with a name that would put Lorenzo's on the map.

'You have worked as a maître d' or restaurant hostess before.'

One slim shoulder lifted. 'My grandmother had an Italian restaurant in an inner-city suburb of Melbourne.'

Melbourne, Australia? *That* was her accent.

'My cousin and I started bussing tables when we were just nine or ten. We loved it.'

He imagined a child version of this woman, lip caught between her teeth as she collected plates, just as it had when she'd parked her van. He could almost see the proud nonna standing nearby, and the restaurant patrons charmed by the enchanting child.

Of course, he expected he imagined for her far lovelier memories than they were in reality, and certainly lovelier than he'd had himself, but the way her lips lifted told him the memory was a fond one, so maybe his imagination wasn't too far wrong.

She shook her head, those blue eyes dancing.

Something inside of him tightened before instantly relaxing, but then those eyes met his and everything tightened again twice as hard. His pulse accelerated with a speed that would do an Italian sportscar proud.

'Over the years, our roles there evolved. I was always drawn to front of house—waitressing and hostessing—while Audrey would head straight for the kitchen. Now if Audrey were here, she'd do an admirable job filling in as your temporary chef.'

'Audrey, however, is not here.' Despite the strange constriction in his throat, his voice emerged smoothly enough. 'You are, and it appears that you could do an admirable job as Lorenzo's maître d'.'

She stepped back, her face falling. '*Me*?'

'You just proved—' he waved at the table where she'd seated her hypothetical guests '—how suited you are to the position.' With her warmth and charm, she would be perfect.

He made some calculations, mentally shuffled his plans to fit the new criteria. Frankie had experience plus she'd clearly enjoyed working at her nonna's restaurant. *And* she spoke fluent Italian.

He *would* save Lorenzo's from the disaster of a false start. Failure was not an option. He needed to honour the man who had saved him and his family. He was determined to pay homage where it was due.

He glanced back at Frankie. 'Your grandmother is Italian?'

'Was,' she murmured. 'She recently passed away.'

His heart grew heavy at the sadness in her eyes. He had to fight the urge to pull her into his arms and comfort her as he would one of his sisters. 'I am very sorry for your loss.'

'Thank you.'

But that happy light had bled from her face, and his temples pounded as he belatedly registered her lack of enthusiasm to work in his restaurant. *Why?* She had said she was here to pick grapes, but the job he was offering her was ten times better. 'Is your grief too fresh? Will working in my restaurant make you feel your grandmother's absence more keenly?'

She opened her mouth, then closed it, frowned. 'This trip to Italy…well it's because of my grandmother that I'm here and…' She folded her arms. 'Working as maître d' wasn't part of the plan.'

'What is the plan?' What was she hoping to achieve? If he could help her achieve it, perhaps she would help him in return?

'For the six weeks I'm here at Riposo, I plan to do whatever odd jobs Senor Silva asks of me before the grape-picking starts. In my spare time I'm going to explore the area. After that I mean to travel wherever the mood takes me.'

It took a superhuman effort to stop his lip from curling. Her nonna had left her a legacy and she was squandering it on an extended holiday? 'May I ask how old you are?'

She blinked. 'Twenty-six.'

Bah! She was too old to be squandering her life, and her grandmother's fortune, in such an irresponsible fashion. Irresponsible *and* immature. He'd sworn to avoid such people at all costs.

Her gaze narrowed. 'Why are you looking at me like that?'

But saying as much would not win her cooperation. It was none of his business what she did with her money. It was none of his business what her grandmother might think of her granddaughter's behaviour. Still, Frankie's nonna had clearly worked hard all of her life. Why hadn't Frankie learned from that example? Why hadn't she—

He pulled in a breath, focussed on the problem at hand. 'It is very important to me that Lorenzo's is a success. I want the restaurant to gain an international reputation for being one of the best restaurants in all of Tuscany. I want people to flock here from far and wide.'

Her nose wrinkled. 'It has to be *the best*?'

Nothing else would do. Lorenzo had thrown Dante, his mother and sisters a lifeline when they'd most needed it. Dante had worked all the hours of the day since to achieve what he had. He would never squander it. He would never stop being grateful for it. And he would pay Lorenzo back the only way he knew how.

'Signor Alberici—'

'Dante,' he said automatically, but then wondered why. He rarely invited employees to refer to him by his first name, unless he worked with them daily like Michael.

She moistened her lips. 'Is it usual for you to personally oversee a project like this?'

'Some projects I decide to oversee myself.'

Her gaze dwelled on his jaw, moved to his throat, and then his shoulders. Her mouth tightened and things inside of him tightened too. Women did not usually look at him like this when appraising him. Women usually found him attractive.

'I hope you don't stress this much about every project or you'll end up with an ulcer.'

What did this woman know about stress? 'My health is none of your concern.' He thrust out his jaw. He knew he must look insufferably haughty, but who did this woman think she was, questioning him like this?

She took a step back. 'No, of course it isn't.'

This was going all wrong! He wanted to win her cooperation, not alienate her. He pulled in a measured breath. 'The loss of Eleanora is a blow. It is going to take time for me to find a suitable replacement. With me working the kitchen and you working front of house, it will give me the breathing space I need to sort things out.'

She waved her hands in front of her face. 'But maître d' *won't* be a hard role to fill.'

Frankie might think it would be easy to train someone for the position, but she was wrong. She had something unique—an air or aura that would be impossible to replicate. Lorenzo's diners would love her. 'Why waste time finding someone else when you have already demonstrated your competence?'

Her continued—and *obvious*—reticence had his temper flaring. 'Have you always been such a restless gadabout?' he demanded, slamming his hands to his hips.

Her eyes widened and she stared at him for several beats, not saying anything. Then she clapped a hand to her mouth, as if to halt a bark of laughter. Those irrepressible eyes danced and he waited rather fatalistically for her to call him stuffy or pompous or something equally unflattering. She didn't. Which was just as well, because if she had, he'd have had to dismiss her. Eventually she just pulled her hand from her mouth and said nothing.

He reached for the threads of his temper. He could order her to take on the role, he was her employer for the next six weeks after all. But ultimatums rarely produced satisfactory results.

'The harvesting of the grapes will not take place for several weeks yet, so why not take this opportunity that presents itself to you? It might not be part of your plan, but it is an exciting and interesting opportunity.'

'The grape picking and odd-jobbing was part-time. I suspect this will be full-time. I'm not interested in working full-time.'

He breathed in through his nose and out through his mouth. 'Lorenzo's is only doing a dinner service. And for the first month we are only open Thursday through Sunday.'

She blinked as if his words had taken the wind out of the sails of her protests.

'As you heard earlier, we open this Saturday night. This week we do have staff training, but again it is only a few hours here and there.'

'You want me to do this instead of the odd-jobbing and grape picking?'

He gave a hard nod. He wanted her focussed wholly on the restaurant. 'What do you say, Frankie, will you be maître d' for a month until I can find a replacement chef? You will earn twice as much money than you would picking grapes. That will ensure you have plenty of money to continue your travels when you leave here—meaning less working and more holiday.'

Perfect lips pursed.

'You are on a working holiday, yes? Consider this one of those unexpected things that happen when one travels overseas—an adventure.'

Her eyes suddenly brightened. 'Can I still camp in Bertha as arranged?'

'Bertha?'

'My van.'

She had named her van? 'All of your former arrangements will stand.'

'Fine.' She rolled her eyes ceilingward. 'You have a deal.'

He tried to not feel affronted at her lack of enthusiasm. There were people who would jump at the opportunity to be front of house at his restaurant.

'You will give me your best work, yes?' His hands slammed to his hips. 'You do not mean to sigh, roll your eyes heavenward and make my patrons feel they are a chore.'

She straightened. 'Of course not. You have my word.'

But what was the word of a restless gadabout worth? He would need to keep a close eye on Frankie Weaver. He refused to let anything else go wrong in the lead up to Lorenzo's opening.

Yes, he'd keep a *very* close eye on Frankie.

CHAPTER TWO

'C, C, F, F, G... C, C, F, F, G...'

Frankie sang the notes over and over, trying to fix them in her mind, while madly strumming on Saffy—her ukulele—and doing all she could to channel the Beatles 'Twist and Shout'. She suspected it sounded better in her head than it did in reality, but what did that matter? She was having *fun*!

Glancing out of Bertha's wide-open back window, she grinned and kicked her heels against the mattress. Look at her lounging on the bed in her sky-blue retro Kombi, with all the splendour of a Tuscan vineyard spread before her, while playing her ukulele. If there was a better picture of holiday indolence, she didn't know what it could be.

Oh, and to make matters even better? Dante had called her a gadabout. *Her?* He thought her an unreliable flake. Nobody had *ever* accused her of that before. She grinned so hard her cheeks started to hurt.

The sudden freedom from having to be responsible and sensible, the freedom from the weight of other people's expectations…the freedom of not being Dr Weaver, made her lift her ukulele in the air in a victory salute.

Unbidden, her father's face rose in her mind. *'Dr Weaver, is this really the best use of your time?'*

Her smile faded and her heart plummeted. For as long as she could remember, she'd wanted to be a doctor. It had felt like what she was supposed to do with her life. It had felt right.

Until her father had died. And she'd promised to follow in his footsteps.

She stared out at grapevines and golden hills and blue sky. Let out a long breath. The joy had slowly bled from that dream, she now acknowledged. Duty had replaced passion. Now whenever she thought about choosing her medical specialty, it felt like a prison sentence.

You promised!

A lump lodged in her throat. How did she reconcile the promise she'd made with the growing certainty that she wanted to be a mother? She couldn't be the mother she wanted to be *and* be the surgeon her father had been.

She hugged Saffy to her chest. She wanted to be present in her child's life. *Very* present. One day she hoped to be like her nonna—wise, loving…the heart of the family. Giving up that dream would…

Her lungs cramped and her breath came in short sharp gasps.

Don't hyperventilate. Stop thinking about it. Three months.

Grabbing Saffy, she launched into her 'C, C, F, F, G' routine until some of the tightness eased from her and she could breathe again. She huffed out a wry laugh. Maybe one day she'd prescribe the ukulele to her patients.

If you're still a doctor.

Gritting her teeth, she strummed on Saffy for all she was worth.

A shadow passed along the wall of her van and she followed it, waiting to see who would appear, blinking when Dante materialised at Bertha's wide-open back window.

She halted mid strum, considered leaping to her feet—though, one had to be careful leaping in the close confines of the van—and then remembered he thought her a *'restless gadabout'*, and resisted the urge. For the next three months, she *wanted* to be the person he thought her. She had every intention of channelling that person for all she was worth.

'*Ciao*, Dante.'

'Hello, Frankie.'

They stared at each other for a moment and she registered the shadows in his eyes, the tight set of his shoulders as if he were constantly braced against some vast invisible weight, and bit back a sigh. If ever a person needed a holiday, it was Dante.

He glanced beyond, clearly curious about the van's setup.

'Come around,' she gestured to the sliding door at the side, 'and see it properly.'

He did as she bid. She currently had the sofa folded down as a bed, and lounged on it crosswise with Saffy negligently held between her hands. He took her in with barely a glance, and then gazed at her tiny hotplates and sink. The cupboards above.

'It's cute, isn't it?'

She shuffled down the bed, handed him Saffy, and then demonstrated how the bed folded into a sofa. For some reason it seemed more comfortable to not have a bed in the vicinity when Dante was nearby. She didn't want to give off *those* kinds of casual vibes.

She showed him how the table folded out, before slotting it back into place, and making shooing gestures so she could exit the van without bumping into him.

The van had an awning which she'd pulled out, and beneath it rested two camp chairs and a wooden crate that served as a coffee table. She waved him to one of the seats now. 'Soda?'

He blinked. 'I…'

She took that as a yes, and set two cans of soda on the wooden crate.

He held her ukulele out towards her and a thread of mischief wormed through her. She folded her arms and stared at him. 'You're here to talk about work, right?'

'I am.'

'Even though I don't officially start work until tomorrow.'

He started to rise. '*Si*, I am impinging on your leisure time.'

'Sit down, Dante. I'm happy to talk work if you humour me.'

'Humour you how?'

She had no idea what devil was prompting her, but it felt carefree and fun, and it wouldn't hurt anyone. 'Dante, meet Saffy.' She gestured to the ukulele he still held. 'Saffy, meet Dante.'

'You name your van Bertha and your ukulele Saffy?'

'It's short for Saffron.' Because Saffy was the hottest of bright oranges. She reached inside the van and pulled out a second ukulele. 'And this is Leilani, the ukulele I've always aspired to play well.' Made from beautiful Hawaiian koa wood, a gorgeous beach scene had been painted onto its surface—a still lagoon and the setting sun framed by a palm tree. 'It's a work of art, don't you think?'

For the first time since she'd met him, his lips twitched with genuine humour. 'It is not exactly what I would call a Raphael or Michelangelo.'

She held Leilani at arm's length and surveyed her. 'No, I believe this is of a school all its own.'

Her nonsense was greeted with a warm chuckle that made her pulse hitch.

'How am I to humour you, Frankie?'

For the briefest of moments her mind flashed to

him stretched out naked on the bed behind her. Her tongue stuck to the roof of her mouth. She gulped and coughed and tried to get her mind back on track. Men were strictly off the agenda until she had her life worked out. She wasn't letting any man influence the decisions she had to make this summer.

Ha! As if Dante would be interested in a woman like her anyway. Her sudden awareness was nothing more than a result of his gorgeous Italian accent and the fact that with his whisky and smoke voice Dante could be an audio book narrator. Her imagination had gone into overdrive, that was all. She wasn't in the market for that kind of holiday fun.

Are you sure?

Ignoring that traitorous inner voice, she gestured at Saffy, refusing to notice how gently he clasped the neck of the ukulele. As if it were precious. She could imagine those fingers—

Oh, no you can't!

'Have you ever played the ukulele before?'

One dark eyebrow rose.

That looked like a no then. This close, she could see his eyes were the darkest of browns—like coffee beans—all smoke and spice. 'Well, I'm here to tell you that it's fun—ridiculous fun—to play a ukulele.'

'And this is why you play?'

'Absolutely. I'm going to show you a couple of chords and—'

'Why?'

He didn't ask in a mean or even impatient way. He was simply perplexed.

She lowered Leilani back to her lap and stared at him. 'Don't you ever do things just for fun?'

He shifted. 'Of course.'

She wasn't convinced. Though maybe opening restaurants and making money *was* his idea of fun.

'So...' His brow pleated. 'This is just for fun?'

'Partly.'

'And the other part?'

'We're going to be working together for the next month?'

He nodded, tension vibrating from him.

He *really* needed to relax. She lifted her ukulele 'This will show me if you're easy to work with or not.'

Those brows shot up. 'You think you will be able to tell what kind of employer I'll be by making me learn a few chords on the ukulele?'

'Absolutely. Now ready?'

For the next ten minutes she showed him four chords and then a strum pattern. Once he had the strum pattern mastered, she called out the chord changes, and when he'd found the rhythm, she started singing 'You Are My Sunshine'.

He stumbled in surprise, so she began calling out the chords again, and when she next started singing, he maintained the pace and pattern, even humming along. And when the song came to an end, his lips broke into the largest of smiles.

'*Dio!* I played a song—a whole song!'

She grinned back, wanting to leap to her feet and dance under the awning as energy poured through her. 'See? It's fun!'

He stared at the ukulele in amazement, then Frankie. 'Thank you.'

His simple gratitude made her chest ache. 'You're welcome. Anytime you want another lesson, you know where to find me.'

She took the ukuleles and stowed them back inside Bertha, and the wistful expression in his eyes made her smile. 'One can learn basic ukulele very quickly, and that means you get to noodle around on your own and feel halfway accomplished.'

'*You* are very good,' he observed.

'I'm terrible! But I'm improving every day and I'm having a ball doing it, and that's the main thing. Learning to play is a joy rather than a stress or…' She trailed off with a shrug, taking her seat again. 'So, Dante, it's your turn now. What did you want to talk to me about?'

He immediately sobered. 'I am uneasy. I cannot lie. I sensed your… I won't call it reluctance, but your lack of enthusiasm to act as maître d'.'

When he didn't say more, it was her turn to shift and fidget. 'And you want to assure yourself that I will give you my best work rather than a half-hearted devil-may-care, "Oh, my God, I'm at work and when does my shift end?" kind of attitude.'

His brow pleated. She had an urge to reach across and smooth it out. Or to push a ukulele into his hands again and make him play another song.

'I would like to know why, when you're clearly very good with people, and made such a great case for how well suited you were to such a position, that you would prefer to be picking grapes and doing menial chores than working in a lovely restaurant with happy people and a beautiful view?'

And just like that he got to the heart of the problem. While also making an attractive case for working in the restaurant. He made it sound like a wonderful job rather than an onerous obligation.

It was just… She'd come to Tuscany to avoid responsibility. She was supposed to be relaxing and unwinding and clearing her mind. Not landing herself with the weight of someone else's expectations to be *the best*.

But telling him that would lead to questions, which would mean giving explanations. And that would change his view of her as a *restless gadabout*, and she didn't want that. When people learned she was a doctor, their attitude towards her changed. For the next three months she wanted to be unremarkable and anonymous.

'My vision of a working holiday was picking grapes in golden fields under a warm sun.' She shrugged. 'I was sad to lose that vision.'

'If you wish it, I will ensure you still get the chance to pick grapes. Though I think that maybe you have romanticised this. It is sweaty physical work.'

Which sounded like heaven to her at the moment.

'And are not working holidays about adventure and having new experiences?'

Which had been the only part of his earlier argument that had carried weight with her.

'One day when Lorenzo's is a world-renowned restaurant with a Michelin star and Eleanora is gnashing her teeth that she cannot count it as a feather to put into her cap, you will be able to say that you were the restaurant's very first maître d' and had a hand in making the restaurant what it has become.'

His vision of grandeur made her laugh. 'You like to dream big.'

'It is the only way to dream.'

A position as maître d' wasn't what she'd envisaged when planning her trip, but maybe she was looking at this wrong. She'd been thinking she needed mindless work that would let her mind rest and be free, but new experiences would renew her too, just in a different way.

Maybe this job would help her find the answers she needed too? If not, it *was* only temporary, the work still only part-time. Even if it wasn't all fun and games, at least she wouldn't be working in a hospital in charge of people's lives where a split-second decision could mean the difference between life and death.

She met his gaze, sensed the anxiety eating at him behind those dark eyes. 'Lorenzo's means a lot to you.'

'It does.'

'Who is Lorenzo.'

'My grandfather.'

Oh!

'I wish to honour his memory.'

And just like that, every hard thing inside her melted. 'What a lovely thing to do. When did you lose him?'

'Last summer.'

She missed Nonna every single day. It was clear he missed his grandfather every bit as much.

'Dante, I'm sorry about my lack of enthusiasm. I didn't mean to be rude. You took me by surprise, that's all. I loved the vision I had in my mind and I didn't want to change it, but you're right—there'll be time for picking grapes under a Tuscan sun. I'd be delighted to act as your maître d' until you can find a new chef.'

Some of the tension in his shoulders eased. 'Thank you.' And then the briefest of smiles curved his lips. 'And now I should like to know what it was you learned from teaching me 'You Are My Sunshine' on the ukulele.'

She'd been surprised when he'd submitted to

the lesson without argument. She knew it had been motivated by his desire to win her cooperation, but he'd also given it his best. He'd given her what he hoped to get back from her in return—*her* best.

'I learned you're not a tyrant or a despot,' she said. 'I wasn't looking forward to working with someone like that, but thankfully that's not something I need to worry about.'

He started to draw himself up, as if unsure whether to be affronted or not, but a moment later his lips twisted. 'Ah, my temper tantrum in the kitchen, it gave you a bad impression.'

She shrugged. 'I don't like to be yelled at.'

Those eyes widened. 'I was not yelling at you! I would not yell at you!'

'You're yelling now.'

His mouth opened and closed, and then he glared at her. 'I will treat you with respect, Frankie. I treat all my employees with respect.'

'And I'll treat you with respect too, Dante. But if you yell at me, I might just yell back.'

'No yelling!'

'Fine by me!' she shot back at exactly the same volume.

He rose, eyes flashing. 'Thank you for your assurances that you will work hard. You have put my mind at rest.'

'Thank you for playing the ukulele with me.'

He turned to go but swung back. 'You are a most unusual woman.'

She grinned. 'I'm going to take that as a compliment.'

With a huff, he stalked away, and she grabbed Saffy and sent him off with 'You Are My Sunshine' ringing in his ears.

She glanced down when her phone started ringing. Biting back a sigh, she pressed it to her ear and made her voice super cheerful. 'Hi, Mum, did you just get the picture of the glorious view I'm currently enjoying?'

Dante watched from the door of the kitchen as Frankie put the waitstaff through their paces. He'd personally chosen each and every member of the team. He wanted only the best for Lorenzo's. It was what his grandfather deserved.

But he had to curl a hand around the door to keep from striding through it and taking over from Frankie. Not that he thought she was doing anything wrong. It was just...

This was *his* restaurant and he wanted to run it *his* way.

In a faraway part of his brain, he knew his attitude was ludicrous, not to mention counterproductive. If he attempted to micromanage every tiny detail, he would alienate his staff. He needed to trust them to do the jobs he'd employed them for.

He just hadn't realised it'd be this difficult.

As if sensing him there, Frankie turned, those clear blue eyes spotlighting him. He felt suddenly and uncomfortably seen.

Dio. He was losing his mind. He had to find a way to manage all of his anxiety about the restaurant. He had to find a way to maintain a sense of proportion. Because Frankie was not the kind of woman who could see inside of another's soul. She might be personable and charming, but she had no depth, no direction, none of the things that gave one the ability to see below the surface into other people's hearts.

He swallowed. Frankie was like his father.

He'd seen the heartache his mother had suffered at his father's hands. He wasn't wishing that on himself. He wouldn't wish it on anyone!

One laughed and had fun with the Frankies and Riccardos of the world. They played ukuleles with them, and hired them for temporary positions, which suited their short attention spans and their wanderlust. The one thing they didn't do was try to see more depth and complexity in them than existed.

And yet Frankie's eyes seem to recognise every chafe and worry in his soul.

She waved him over. 'Why don't you join us, Dante?' Then before he could either decline or accept her invitation, she turned back to the waitstaff. 'Everyone, this is Signor Dante Alberici, who owns the vineyard and restaurant.'

She dimpled cheekily as he moved across to where she stood and he wondered if she ever managed to maintain a semblance of seriousness for ten minutes straight.

'Apparently Signor Alberici has a secret passion for cooking, which I confess I'm looking forward to sampling. He's Lorenzo's head chef for the foreseeable future.'

He gave a brief nod. *'Buongiorno.'*

A rush of *buongiornos* were murmured back to him, along with wide-eyed stares. It was clear they hadn't expected to meet the tycoon himself.

He felt suddenly awkward, as if he didn't belong here. *Dio!* Riposo *was* his home. It was the one place where he *did* belong.

'Have you ever waited tables before, Dante?'

Frankie's words hauled him back and he shook his head. 'When I was at university I had part-time jobs in construction—building houses and apartments. I have never worked front of house in a restaurant.'

She blinked, frowned, then shook herself. 'Would you like to give it a try?'

He who *was* a good judge of character and *did* have the ability to see below other people's surfaces, couldn't work out if she wanted him to accept or decline her invitation.

He wavered momentarily. *What would you like to do?* His back straightened. 'Yes, I would like that very much.'

For the next two hours Dante found himself setting tables, taking mock orders, delivering dishes of pretend food to the tables. Frankie created scenarios, acting the role of the paying customer, and then asking the staff what they would do. 'Could I get a booster seat for my toddler and some crayons for my little girl, so she can draw while we eat our meal.'

Cavolo! He hadn't factored children in at all. This might be a winery, but of course some patrons would have children with them when they came to dine. He made a mental note to research that further.

'A couple arrives and the woman is crying. You've seen the man slap her in the car park. What do you do?'

His every muscle stiffened. He—

'First of all, when they come inside, you point out to the woman where the washroom is, and you send a female member of staff in after her to check if she needs help or needs you to call the police. We have a code word in Australian bars—Angela. If a woman comes up to the bar and asks if Angela is there, it means she needs help. There are usually posters in the women's bathrooms explaining how this works. Sometimes she needs the police to be called, other times she might just need a discreet exit.'

They would do this! They would—

'This is a restaurant, not a nightclub or bar where

a woman might be approached by a strange man who frightens her, so a poster like that isn't necessary here. Two things to remember in this situation, though—the first is we're not to play hero. Starting a brawl in the restaurant won't help anyone. Also, the woman may simply tell you to mind your own business, and you need to accept her decision. It is our duty as reasonable human beings to ask the question and offer assistance, nothing more.'

He wanted to rail and rage against this cold-hearted pragmatism. He wanted to tell Frankie that he wouldn't countenance violence against women on his premises. He—

'Now, Lorenzo's is the kind of restaurant where the waitstaff need to familiarise themselves with the menu. And with Dante here, we're lucky enough to have the opportunity to ask him any questions we might have in relation to said menu.'

Nobody opened their mouth to ask him anything. While they'd welcomed him with smiles and he sensed they enjoyed having him work alongside them, he still clearly intimidated them.

Frankie picked up a menu. 'Okay, Dante, my customer is trying to decide between the lamb and the chicken pasta. What advice can I give her?'

He straightened. *Now* he was in his element. 'If she prefers strong savoury flavours she should choose the lamb, while the chicken has a more delicate flavour and a creamier texture which might be more to her liking.'

A waitress turned to him. 'I strongly dislike the taste of mushrooms, but I know many people love them. How would you recommend I describe a dish that includes mushrooms as a main ingredient?'

He couldn't help but smile at her hesitant earnestness. 'By not curling up your nose or looking as if you've sucked on a lemon when you mention the word mushrooms.'

She along with everyone else laughed. He then went on to explain how he would focus on the flavours in the dish that the mushrooms were a vehicle for.

He had several other questions, one related to food intolerances and another about the restaurant's stance on customers who requested changes to a listed dish. He answered them easily, and finished by assuring all of the staff that they were always welcome to seek him out in the kitchen to check if such changes could be accommodated.

Before he was either aware or ready for it, the induction and training session was over. The two hours had flown by! He found, though, that his anxieties had calmed. Instead, of feeling restless and tense, a growing optimism flooded his veins. He could rest easy in the knowledge that his front of house staff *were* friendly, efficient and knew what they were doing.

He pushed his shoulders back. Lorenzo's would be a success, and a fitting tribute to his grandfather for all of his kindness—for picking up the reins of familial duty where his father had not.

Movement from the corner of his eye had him blinking himself back into the present. With easy economical movements, Frankie straightened the menus and placed them in their spot on the maître d' stand. She turned to him with a smile. 'That went well. Wouldn't you agree?'

'*Si*, yes. Thank you for asking me to join you.'

One corner of her mouth lifted. 'Well, we couldn't have you spending the entire time bristling in the doorway and glaring at us as if daring us to make a mistake now, could we?'

'I wasn't—'

'Was too.'

She planted her hands on her hips. Very nice hips. They flared gently from a slender waist. Her fitted button-down blouse hinted at generous curves there as well. His mouth dried. Moistening his lips, he forced his gaze back to her face.

'You were clearly itching to be out here, to reassure yourself the staff were competent and things will be fine on the night.'

She had read him like a book. He had been too transparent. It did not do to wear one's heart on their sleeve. Lorenzo's meant a great deal to him, but it would be foolhardy to advertise that fact so explicitly.

'But now you're happy with your staff. You're no longer so worried. That has to be a good thing.'

'I am very happy with the staff.' It took all his strength not to frown. 'You were very good too.'

'Thank you,' she said just as gravely, though he couldn't help thinking she was laughing at him behind her momentary and uncharacteristically solemn demeanour.

'You remembered everybody's names.' It had amazed him.

'I have a very good memory.' And then she winked, shattering the solemnity. 'It's one of my many talents.'

He didn't doubt that she was blessed with a multitude of talents. And yet she was wasting them all, travelling around in a camper van with her ukulele instead.

'How did you find being a waiter?'

'It was not as easy as I thought it would be.'

'No.'

His eyes narrowed. 'You *wanted* me to find it challenging.'

She frowned then too. 'If you understand the challenges your waitstaff face, it will make you a better maître d'.'

It was odd to discover that he wanted the playful, dancing, blue-eyed laughter back. He thrust out his chin. 'You do not think I will be a good maître d'?'

'I'm sure you'll be fabulous at it.'

'But?'

Her frown deepened. 'Have you ever done it

before, Dante? Are you planning to be Lorenzo's full-time maître d'? It's clear that the restaurant means a lot to you, and it just makes me wonder why you haven't hired someone experienced for the position?'

'This is of no concern of yours!'

She blinked and took a step back. 'You're right, I'm sorry. That was out of line.'

Which left him feeling like an absolute heel. 'No, it is I who should apologise. You have, how do you say it, scraped me on my sore spot? For the summer, this is what I planned—to be Lorenzo's maître d'. I thought having me here as the face of the restaurant would add a touch that is personal and make the customers feel special and welcome and want to come back. I have a name that is recognised and I wanted to trade on that to bring in diners.'

'All very laudable.'

'But you were very busy behind the scenes, recognising potential problems and averting them. You have made me see that the job is not as straightforward as I thought it would be.'

On every step of this project, he'd allowed emotion to override reason. He needed to find a way to keep it in check. He'd never embark on a warehouse conversion or a housing development in such a fashion. He'd reprimand any of his project managers for doing so. Pulling out a chair, he sat heavily at the nearest table. Frankie hesitated, before sitting too.

'Dante, *you* are the boss. You have all the wealth and power in the world.'

That is not what it felt like to him. He had money, yes, and money meant security. It meant that he could ensure his mother and sisters would always be taken care of, that they would never have to suffer the hardships and indignities of the past again.

'*You* get to decide the role you want here at Lorenzo's. It's *your* restaurant.'

He lifted his head to meet that warm blue-eyed gaze. She wasn't laughing at him now. She was staring at him as if she could see into the very secret heart of him and liked what she saw. 'You can be the host without having to perform any of the other duties associated with maître d'.'

He straightened. She was right.

She sent him one of those carefree grins. 'You get to set the tone and atmosphere, you get to choose the menus and the wine list, and you get to hire the right staff to make sure everything runs exactly how you want it to.'

She made it sound so simple.

It was that simple.

Somehow, he'd made it complicated.

Because emotion was complicated.

He forced himself to his feet. 'I will advertise

for a new maître d' at once. But until then, you are still happy to perform the role?'

'Yes.'

'Did anything in today's session worry you or give you concerns.'

'Only the one.'

'What's that?'

'Me, Dante.'

He sat again. 'But you were superb.'

'Oh, I'm good with people. I enjoy the hustle and bustle of a restaurant. But...'

But what?

She dropped her head to her arms with a groan. 'I don't know wine.'

She didn't know...

'Nonna's restaurant was BYO.' She lifted her head. 'We had house red and house white and that was it.'

'*Dio.* This is sacrilege!'

She shrugged. 'It was a cheap and cheerful family restaurant. Good food and a casual atmosphere in an inner-city suburb. Nonna's had no pretensions of grandeur.'

He shot to his feet. 'This needs to be rectified immediately.'

CHAPTER THREE

A LIGHT FLARED in Dante's espresso-dark eyes, his body vibrating with…

Frankie frowned and studied his powerful frame. Not with feminine appreciation, but with a practised, clinical eye. Well, okay, she *almost* managed that. Even as a doctor, it was impossible not to admire such masculine perfection.

The tension, Frankie. You're supposed to be assessing stress levels.

She snapped back, doing her best to observe rather than appreciate. Dante crackled with an excess of energy, but it didn't draw all his muscles tight or darken his eyes as it had earlier when he'd stared at her and the rest of the waitstaff from the door of the kitchen.

That, at least, was something.

It was clear, though, that honouring his grandfather's memory meant a lot to him. Still, she doubted his grandfather would want it to adversely affect his grandson's health. And if Dante wasn't careful, his health would suffer.

This is none of your concern.

As he'd already told her. She ground her teeth together. *This* was why she wanted to be grape picking on a hillside somewhere. Then she wouldn't be worrying about stuff like this.

Brows lowered over those dark eyes. 'Why do you huff out such a loud sigh?'

Oh! She hadn't meant to. 'It's just I can't help thinking you should hire someone who has all the appropriate knowledge of the wines you offer here, rather...'

'Rather...?'

'Than a restless gadabout like me.' As she said the words, she couldn't stop her heart from dancing a delighted jig. What a joy that thought was.

'You promised me a month. Are you telling me your word is not to be trusted?'

The tension that now had him in its grip was of the jaw-clenching kind and she sobered. 'Of course not. I'll keep my promise.'

Restless gadabout lost a little of its glamour. It was fun to be thought of as a free spirit, but not if he thought it made her unreliable. She wanted to reduce her own stress levels, not add to anyone else's.

'Look, your restaurant clearly means a lot to you. I don't relish the thought of being the weak link in the chain.'

Her words had him shaking his head. 'You are not a weak link. You are...'

She found herself leaning forward as if hanging on his every word. She forced herself back in her seat, slouched and tried to channel laid-back and casual.

'You are an unexpected bonus,' he finally pronounced. 'You are at home in this world.' He gestured around the dining room. 'You are charming and fun and set a tone I want for my restaurant. The wine thing? *Pffi!*'

His pronouncement startled a laugh from her. 'I think this is where I remind you that Riposo is a winery. People will expect fine wines as part of the dining experience. They'll expect the staff to make knowledgeable recommendations.'

'I can teach you everything you need to know?'

Her heart leaped at the thought. And her pulse. *Be sensible.* She did what she could to channel visions of a Tuscan hillside and grapevines and the sun, but the vision kept slipping out of reach. She stretched her neck first one way then the other. Learning about wine could be fun.

'Come.'

Reaching down, he took her hand and pulled her to her feet. And just as it had yesterday, when they'd shaken hands for that brief moment, an electric charge skittered across the surface of her skin.

He, however, seemed utterly unaware of it as he led her through to the other end of the building and the wine tasting area, where polished cement floors, vaulted ceilings and a long wooden bar greeted them. Seating her on a stool, he moved behind the bar and pulled forth a selection of wines. At the other end of the bar a woman performed the same ritual for a group of six, and halfway along the bar a couple relaxed on stools, glasses of wine clasped in their hands.

It was clean, professional and… She searched for the appropriate description, but before she could she grew aware of the weight of Dante's stare. 'What?'

'I was trying to work out what you were thinking. The expression on your face…'

'Curiosity. This is the first winery I've ever been inside.'

'But Australia has some world-renowned wineries.'

They did. She just hadn't visited any of them. There were a lot of things she hadn't done. Pushing the thought aside, she stared around again. 'I was trying to find the right word to describe the atmosphere. I mean it's very clean, almost clinical.' At a pinch, she'd bet one could operate on a patient in here.

'If you think this is clean, you ought to see the room where we ferment the wine in vats. It is a scientific business, this making of good wine.'

She didn't doubt that for a moment. 'And yet it's also relaxing too. One can walk through those doors and feel as if they're on holiday.'

He murmured a beautiful-sounding Italian

curse. 'I did not think. This is your leisure time. I am once again impinging on—'

'I'll make a deal with you, Dante.'

'You are a big one for making deals.'

'I'll let you teach me what I need to know about wine in my leisure time, if you'll relax a bit more.'

He frowned. 'How do you wish me to do this? Does it involve a ukulele?'

'Now there's a thought!'

She grinned. He didn't grin back, but a ghost of a smile curved his lips. It gave her hope that she could actually get him to unwind a bit. Maybe it would be possible to delay that prospective ulcer yet.

'I'll show you what I mean.'

Reaching out, she unknotted his tie and undid his top button. The breath whistled between his teeth, the sound angling straight to her core. Something warm and sweet woke inside her, stretching and yearning. She gulped. Dear God, this had been a mistake. She hadn't meant to make this suggestive or seductive. Pulling back now, though, would mean betraying herself, making things even more awkward.

Swallowing, she slipped the tie from his collar. It seemed to take forever. Gritting her teeth, she kept going with dogged determination until she reached the end. Did Dante *have* to wear the longest ties known to man?

'Wrist please.' She used her doctor's voice, hoping it would help her find the equilibrium she desperately needed. Instead, his instant response to the authority she projected had her imagining a different scenario involving a bed, mood lighting and—

Don't go there.

All her years of training kept her fingers deft. As quickly and efficiently as she could, she undid the button on the cuff of his business shirt and rolled the sleeve halfway up his forearm, and then gestured for his other arm. By the time she was finished her heart was racing and perspiration prickled her nape and the secret space between her breasts.

'There!' She clapped her hands. 'That's much better.'

'Better how?' he demanded, his voice full of gravel. He looked as if he'd like to throttle her. She didn't blame him. She'd like to throttle herself!

'Well, for a start,' she gestured at his throat, 'you now look as if you can breathe.'

His fingers went to the column of his throat—tanned, strong and inviting. She sent a silent message for him to undo another button, but he clearly didn't hear it, because that hand clenched and lowered back to the bar.

She dragged her gaze from his throat and folded her arms. 'While the rolled-up shirtsleeves make you look much more casual and approachable.'

He blinked as if the thought of being considered unapproachable had never occurred to him.

'We now look like two friends about to embark on an adventure—a wine tasting adventure.' Except that he glowered at her in a far from friendly fashion. 'Or if not friends, then at least work colleagues having a friendly chat over a glass or two of wine.' That was such a lie and if she were Pinocchio, her nose would've just grown six inches.

He stared at her as if she was mad, and it took all her strength to not reach up and touch her nose, just to make sure it was the same size and shape it always was.

She folded her arms tighter. 'At least this now feels like it could be a fun activity I'd do in my leisure time, rather than a work commitment.'

Liar, liar, pants on fire.

He adjusted his stance. 'And this,' he gestured to himself, 'is me keeping my side of the deal.'

Actually, he looked more wound up and tense than ever. She was clearly just as bad at this relaxation thing as he was. And if he didn't stop glaring at her like that, she had a feeling she might just catch fire on the spot! She glared back. 'Oh, yes, you look *so* relaxed, Dante. The epitome of light-hearted cheer.'

He leaned across the bar towards her and the sudden proximity made her breath catch. 'Then you should not have undressed me in public.' Dark eyes flashed. 'This is not the way to get a person to relax.'

She winced.

'If the tables were turned and I undid several of your buttons, it would be considered entirely inappropriate and sexually predatory. And—'

She reached out and touched her fingers to his mouth. 'I'm sorry,' she whispered.

She reefed her hand away because the touch of his lips against bare flesh burned. She rubbed her fingers against her leg. She'd gone too far and now she didn't know how to make things right again. So much for being carefree and happy-go-lucky! 'It was a ridiculous thing to do. I wasn't thinking. I didn't mean to make things…weird.'

He didn't say anything.

'You were looking so formal and perfect and I wanted to mess you up a little, make you look more human. But I should've asked you to take off your tie and roll up your own shirtsleeves. Will you please accept my apology?'

His frown didn't diminish and his jaw remained clenched.

She recalled his other words and straightened. 'I also want to assure you that I was not trying to make any kind of sexual move on you. You're a wealthy man, not to mention handsome, so you must be used to women throwing themselves at you, but that's not what I was doing.'

Heat flooded her face and she suspected she'd

just turned scarlet, and no amount of medical training could help her counter that. 'I wish the floor would open up and swallow me,' she groaned.

Finally, there was a lightening in those eyes, a relaxation of the jaw. He looked as if he might even be trying to bite back a smile. 'It might have been a thought that did cross my mind,' he said, 'but the look on your face now tells me that it was not so.'

'If I was flirting with you, I hope I could manage it with a bit more finesse.' More heat flooded through her. Though she was so out of practise at flirting, it couldn't be guaranteed.

He nodded, and those dark eyes might've even been dancing. 'You look so uncomfortable now that I cannot help thinking you have been amply punished for your impulsiveness.'

Her heart did a funny little boom-boom at the sight of his lips curving upwards. Swallowing, she nodded towards the bottles lined up on the bar beside them. 'Am I correct in thinking you're not going to now allow me to slink away and have my wine lesson another time?'

'We made a deal.'

She couldn't help but laugh at the way he'd turned the tables on her. 'But you and me, we're okay?' she checked. 'And what just happened— my stupidity—we can pretend it never happened?'

He nodded.

Her entire body sagged. It was more than she deserved and they both knew it. Before he had time to rue his generosity, she gestured towards the wine bottles again. 'Okay, teach me everything I need to know. I want to do Lorenzo's proud.'

'What do you usually drink?'

'I don't really.'

He stared. 'You are a teetotaller?'

'No. And before you ask, I don't have a problem with alcohol. It's just that my parents rarely drank, so it wasn't something I learned about when I was growing up.'

Instead, she'd learned about things like vivisections, pulmonary structures and osteoclasis.

'What do you drink when you go to a bar with friends? What kind of wine do you take to dinner parties?'

She so rarely did either of those things. They belonged to a life she wanted, though. 'If I'm at a bar I usually have a shandy.'

He stared at her as if he had no idea what she was talking about.

'It's half beer, half lemonade.' He made a face so she rushed on. 'And if I'm going to a dinner party, I'll usually take along a bottle of Shiraz.'

'How do you choose this Shiraz?'

He would hate her answer.

'Come, come,' he said as if sensing her reluctance.

'I tell a shop assistant that I want a bottle of

Shiraz for a dinner party and tell them how much money I want to spend.'

He threw his hands up. 'You are so brilliant with food and so clueless about wine.'

He thought her brilliant with food?

He leaned towards her, his eyes alive and determined. 'I am going to teach you how to appreciate wine, to understand how it can complement a meal, and how sharing something you love and appreciate with others—like a good bottle of wine—can make your soul sing.'

The breath left her lungs on a fast exhale, and she sagged against the back of her stool.

'What?' he demanded.

He'd given her a vision she wanted for her future. One where there was time and energy to not just share a meal, but to savour it as well. With people who mattered. She used to do that when she was younger—savoured such things—especially in Nonna's restaurant.

'Frankie?'

But how long had it been since she'd shared such a meal with her family? No wonder Nonna had left her that letter. Had Nonna felt—?

'Frankie?'

A warm hand clasped hers, making her jump.

'Where did you just go? What just happened.'

'When you were talking about wine you sounded like a poet. It made me think of my nonna.' Her throat ached, regrets burning in her belly. 'She would approve of this—of me learning to appreciate wine.'

His gaze raked her face. 'You miss her.'

'With all my heart.'

The expression in Frankie's eyes made Dante's chest burn. He suspected that, like him, she would give everything she owned just to spend another day with her beloved grandparent.

He dragged his gaze from her face. Fixating on luscious lips would be a mistake. As would becoming entranced with hair the colour of caramel that shone in the overhead lights and looked so soft he yearned to reach out and touch it. This woman made him *want* things.

He didn't *want* to want anything. All he wanted to do was keep his focus squarely on ensuring Lorenzo's was a success. The nonsense that had just happened between the two of them should be warning enough to keep him on his guard.

'So which wine are we going to start with?'

In answer, he poured sample-sized portions of prosecco into two glasses, and pushed one towards her.

'Bubbles!' Her smile was wide as she lifted her glass and held it to the light. She slanted him a mischievous glance. 'I've seen how this is done in movies.' She sobered and concentrated and he didn't know if it was a pretence or not. 'I believe this wine is very pale in colour while the bubble count must be in the hundreds of thousands.'

She was doing her best to make him laugh after what had just passed between them, and he should make an effort to play along, dispel the lingering tension, the threat of heat that remained in the air. But his gaze lowered to the fingers holding the wineglass and things inside him clenched as he recalled in precise detail how she'd slipped the tie from his collar, the pull as she'd tugged it free... the fierce and primitive desire that had burned through him, hard and fast and insistent.

He'd wanted to drag her across the bar and kiss her until she was boneless with want and need. The way she'd looked at him had told him that maybe she'd be more than happy for him to do that too.

What had started out as a joke had evolved into something else. Without warning. A deep burning betrayed by parted lips, quick intakes of breath, and hard swallowing. The pulse at the base of her throat had thrashed and fluttered like a wild thing, while deep inside him his blood had pounded too hard, too loud, too fast.

He'd wanted her, with a desperate fierceness he hadn't experienced since he was a teenager. But he was no longer a callow youth. His worry about the restaurant was skewing his judgment, had allowed barriers to fall. He needed to set them firmly in place again.

'I'm guessing that if someone has come to the restaurant to celebrate an anniversary or their birthday, I would suggest a bottle of Riposo's prosecco.'

He snapped back. 'That would be a very good option. If the celebration is an important one the diners wish to mark with something particularly special, our 2012 vintage, while more expensive, is like liquid gold.'

'2012. Liquid gold,' she repeated as if fixing it in her mind.

'Hold the glass to your nose and smell the wine.'

He demonstrated what he meant, but rather than the fruity accents of the prosecco, all he could smell was the warm amber notes of Frankie's scent. There was something else, a lighter note. He inhaled more deeply, searched his memory... *carnation*. Frankie smelled of amber and carnations. Warm, pretty...addictive.

'It smells fruity like peaches or plums.'

'That is the top note. You might also make out hints of honeysuckle and pear.'

He kept his gaze on his own glass as she lifted the glass to her nose again. He didn't want to note how alive her eyes were with interest. He didn't want to imagine those small hands on his body or—

'The way to best taste wine is to take a sip and let the wine coat your tongue, before swallowing.

Then take a couple of smaller sips to try and identify the individual flavours.'

She did as he said, took a sip and held it in her
mouth. She blinked as if…

His chest clenched. She looked as if she were
coming awake.

'This is really lovely.'

'But of course.' He tried to make himself as
haughty as he could, but her words warmed him
too. 'We only make the best at Riposo. Tell me
what you can taste.'

'It's sweeter than I thought it'd be, but not too
sweet.'

'It pairs particularly well with cured meats and
fruit-driven appetisers.'

She laughed. 'Thank you for the hint. I'm
guessing this and the prosciutto-wrapped melon
would be a match made in heaven.'

She was a quick study.

She set her glass back to the bar, glancing at it
a little wistfully, as if she'd like to finish it, but
then at the array of bottles she still had to try and
clearly thinking the better of it.

He touched the spittoon beside them. 'You can
spit it out if you wish.'

'No, thank you.'

She said it a little primly and he bit back a
smile. She might act all carefree and casual, but
the way she'd just said that made him think she
considered spitting the height of bad manners.

Next they sampled the Vermintino, followed by a Pinot Grigio and then a rosé. He told her the kind of foods they would pair well with. Quick as a flash, she'd return with something that was on the menu.

He was impressed at how quickly she'd memorised the menu. She hadn't been bragging when she'd told him she had a good memory. 'Okay, let's see how good you really are? I will make up some new dishes for our menu and I want you to tell me what wine will pair well with them.'

'Game on!' She clapped her hands. 'I love a good challenge.'

Must this woman make a game of everything? Dismissing the thought, he focussed on dishes he would love to one day serve in the fantasy restaurant of his imagination—a restaurant where he was head chef for real rather than a temporary stand-in. He named dishes, describing their main ingredients, and she'd return a rapid-fire suggestion for an appropriate wine.

He stared at her afterwards. She'd had a ninety percent success rate. And she was only a beginner. She hadn't taken umbrage either when he made an alternate suggestion. Instead, he could practically see that good memory of hers filing it all away for future reference.

What a waste! This woman should be putting her significant talents to use, not frittering them away on some frivolous working holiday. She should be making a name for herself somewhere.

Her simple enjoyment of the wine, of learning all about it, though, had things inside of him unclenching. It had been a long time since he'd worked the cellar door. In summers past, he'd spent a lot of time in here, sharing his love of wine with visitors. But he hadn't done that for...

It had to be at least three years, though it was probably longer. The demands of his business had meant he'd grown increasingly busy. Maybe Frankie was right. Maybe one should take the time to remember these simple pleasures.

However, they should not be overtaken by them. One should not squander their time on only enjoying wine or creating a tempting menu or cooking good food. He pulled himself back into straight lines. He would remain practical, clear-eyed... dispassionate.

Frankie, though, was far from dispassionate. She beamed at him. When he noted the glitter in her eyes, he smothered a smile. 'I think perhaps we will save the red wines for another day.

Those lovely blue eyes danced. 'I think that's wise. I told you I'm not much of a drinker, and while I don't think I've drunk that much, I can feel it in my bloodstream.'

'And what would your nonna think of that?' he teased.

'Oh, she'd have loved all of this. She'd be so

happy to know that I was experiencing it.' The dimples in her cheeks deepened. 'She would also approve of me stopping now too,' she added with a laugh. 'It would be very poor form if I was seen weaving among the grapevines trying to find my way back to Bertha.'

The image had him chuckling. 'That would not do at all.'

Her eyes widened and she stared, as if his amusement had caught her off guard. He rolled his shoulders and swallowed. 'Where in Italy was your grandmother from?'

She shook herself. 'Lucca.'

'But that is not forty minutes from here!'

'I know. I'm planning to visit.'

Is that what her holiday was about—to pay homage to her ancestors? 'Is this working holiday of yours about feeling closer to your grandmother?'

She leaned back on her stool, those cool eyes assessing him. Reaching out, she picked up her glass of Pinot Grigio and swirled the golden liquid. He wondered if she was noting the way it coated the glass, how the light reflected through it...or whether it was an absentminded movement and that she herself was far away, thinking of her grandmother.

'She left me a letter.'

He swallowed. He wished Lorenzo had left him a letter.

'She knew she was dying, you see, but she kept it from us right until the end. Said she hadn't wanted to worry us.' She grimaced. 'Cancer.'

He squeezed her hand. 'I'm sorry.' Reluctantly, he pulled his hand back to his side. Given the beast that stirred inside him at such a simple touch, he needed to be very careful around this woman.

'What about you? Did you know Lorenzo was dying?'

He shook his head. 'It was very quick and unexpected. A heart attack.'

'I'm sorry.' They stared at each other in the solidarity of their shared grief and then she shook herself. 'So, yes, she wrote letters to both me and Audrey, her granddaughters. In mine she told me she should like for me to spend a summer in Italy and provided me with a small legacy to do so.' She shrugged. 'So here I am.'

'Did she tell you why?'

She sucked her bottom lip into her mouth and worried at it with her teeth and a desperate hunger clawed through him. All he could think about was turning that mouth up to meet his and exploring every inch of those luscious lips with mouth, tongue and teeth until he'd had his fill, until he tasted her need and swallowed her moans and had them both burning for more. His groin went hard and tight and he cursed himself for such wayward thoughts.

He didn't have time for a woman in his life. He

didn't need or want the distraction or the intrusion on his current time and resources. And if he did, he certainly wouldn't choose someone like Frankie.

Frankie released her lip, shiny and plump, to prop her chin on her hand. He ground his back molars together. 'She wants me to take stock of my life.'

He ground them even harder. Perhaps she'd given her granddaughter the luxury of one final holiday before exhorting her to knuckle down and make something of herself. One couldn't be carefree and irresponsible forever.

'Tell me something about your grandfather.'

He blinked.

'Fair's fair. I just told you about Nonna and why I'm here.'

'Is this another one of your deals?'

'Of course not. You're free to tell me you're a busy man with important things to do and walk away to do them.'

'I am a busy man and I do have many important things to do.'

Like going over the menu one more time before Lorenzo's opened on Saturday night, and checking the stock again, and...

'Thank you, Dante, for teaching me about wine. It was unexpectedly fun. This one,' she lifted the Pinot Grigio and took a final sip, 'is my favourite. And before I leave Tuscany, I'm going to eat in your gorgeous restaurant and pair this with the lemon garlic salmon.'

She smiled at him as she slid off her stool.

'I didn't meet Lorenzo until I was twelve years old.'

The words slipped from him without warning. If she'd harangued and hassled him for a story, he'd have clammed up. Instead, she'd been generous with her praise and had moved to not take up any more of his time. He might not approve of the way she was wasting her life, but frankly that was none of his business. Frankie was a lot of things he might not approve of, but he couldn't deny that she was gracious and charming. And generous.

And it was a surprise to discover that he wasn't yet ready to end their conversation.

CHAPTER FOUR

FRANKIE HAD TAKEN Dante's words about being *'a busy man with many important things to do'* as a dismissal. After her ill-advised attempt to make him look more relaxed, she'd been determined to retreat with dignity.

Questions clamoured through her now, though, as she struggled back onto her stool. She pulled the tiny portion of Pinot Grigio back towards her. She didn't have to drive anywhere today, had nowhere else she needed to be.

Besides, she suspected this heady, dizzy feeling had more to do with Dante than the amount of alcohol running through her bloodstream. Another couple of sips wouldn't hurt her. 'Why didn't you meet Lorenzo until you were twelve?'

He topped up her wine—just another quarter of a glass. It was an absentminded gesture, as if he'd noted the glass was close to empty. It was kind. And oddly nurturing.

Stay focussed.

'We didn't know about each other until then.

My father was illegitimate and his mother had never told him who his father was.'

Wow.

'But when she died, her solicitor contacted Lorenzo and revealed the truth—that an affair they'd had when they were young had resulted in her becoming pregnant with my father.'

'Why didn't she tell him at the time?'

'He'd become engaged to someone else.'

Ouch.

'Was your father happy to meet his father?'

His face closed up and she immediately regretted asking the question.

'My father is an irresponsible gambler who, when he had spent all of our money, abandoned his wife and four children, and left us destitute.' The ice in his voice lifted all the fine hairs on her arms. 'I was seven when I last saw my father. I do not wish to see him again. To the best of my knowledge, Lorenzo never met him either.'

She rubbed a hand across her chest. 'I'm sorry, Dante.'

His chin came up at that haughty angle. 'It is not your fault. You have nothing to apologise for.'

She bit her tongue, but those dark eyes narrowed.

'You have a question?' he asked.

'I have several. But I probably shouldn't ask any of them.'

'I invite you to ask them.'

He sounded so formal and it made her frown. 'Why would you *invite me* to do that?' She didn't mean to sound challenging, but he didn't strike her as the kind of man who encouraged questions about his background.

'Because one can tell a lot about a person from the questions they ask.'

A test? 'Right, like there's no pressure now or anything.'

His lips twitched.

'Though, I also note, you don't promise to answer my questions.'

He laughed, and as the amusement rippled over his face, she again found herself hypnotised by the change in him. The hard lines of his face relaxed, making him look more...human. When guarded—and stressed—he looked like a statue of an angel—beautiful and perfect. But when he let down that guard, he looked like a man full of vitality and passion and the effect was ten times more powerful than the perfection.

'You have more talents than simply your good memory, Frankie.'

She pulled her mind back to their conversation. 'You were seven when your father left, but you said Lorenzo didn't learn about you—or you about him—until you were twelve. You said your father left you penniless. How did your mother make ends meet with four children to support?'

A deep, hard anger flared in his eyes, but she

didn't recoil from it. It wasn't directed at her. 'My mother, my three sisters and I, lived in a three-room hovel in one of the poorest parts of Rome. My mother—' his hands clenched '—worked all the hours of the day, and many nights too, at menial jobs, to keep food in our bellies and a roof over our heads. It took a toll on her health and she developed pneumonia. If Lorenzo hadn't found us when he did, I do not know what we should have done.'

The shadows in his eyes had her throat thickening. 'But he did find you.' It took all her strength not to reach out and clasp his hand. She didn't think he'd welcome the touch.

He poured a little Pinot Grigio for himself, those broad shoulders unhitching a fraction. 'Yes, and I will be grateful for that till my dying day.'

'He loved you from the first?'

Stern lips curved into a smile. 'He was delighted to discover us. He mourned that he had not known about us until that time. His legitimate family, however, were not quite as enthused.'

She winced.

'They refused to meet us or to have anything to do with us.'

'What a shame. They should have been able to forgive him a youthful indiscretion. And it's certainly not as if any of you were to blame.'

One powerful shoulder lifted. 'Family can be complicated.'

She tapped her glass to his. 'Truer words,' she murmured. 'But despite what the rest of his family thought, he helped you leave Rome?'

'He brought us here to Riposo.'

The perfect retreat from a cruel world.

'He made to us a gift of this vineyard, and ensured that nobody could ever take it away from us.'

Nobody being the rest of Lorenzo's resentful family, she guessed. He had given the young Dante and his sisters, not to mention their mother, a priceless gift—a place to call home.

'It allowed my mother to recover her health and live a gentler life.'

The light in his eyes told her how much that had meant to him.

'He gave us four children the means to get a good education, while the profits from the vineyard ensured I could go to university and study business. We owe him *everything*.'

'So *that's* why Lorenzo's is so important to you. *That's* why you've lost so much perspective and have been so driven.'

His nostrils flared. 'I do not lose perspective, as you put it. But, yes, the restaurant is very important to me. I wish it to be a fitting tribute to a good man.'

Hadn't lost perspective? She folded her arms and quoted *verbatim* one of his more colourful insults when he'd discovered that Eleanora Toussaint had let him down. 'It's usual then for you to lose your temper when setbacks happen—to utter insults while waving your arms about in the air and stomping about like a madman?'

He rubbed a hand over his face.

'It's why you hover in doorways when your staff are being trained, like some helicopter parent, glowering at all and sundry, making everyone worry they're not going to measure up?'

'That is not what I was doing today!'

She raised an eyebrow.

'I was merely interested in what was happening and how it was proceeding.'

She raised the other eyebrow.

With a groan he collapsed, elbows on the bar, head in hands. 'What is wrong with me? It is like a madness has gripped me and I can no longer think straight.'

She moved a couple of glasses that were in danger of being knocked over out of the way. 'So ordinarily you're not quite so…passionate?'

'How is it you say?' He lifted his head. 'Cool as a cucumber, that is me.'

'Tell me something lovely about Lorenzo.'

He eased back, the tightness slowly draining from his face. 'He was a man who worked hard, but played hard too. Not in ugly ways, you understand—he wasn't a drinker or a gambler or a womaniser. But he took great joy in good food and good wine and good company. He milked every moment for the joy it held.' He shook his head. 'I had never met anyone like that before.'

Her heart felt suspended between breaths at the warm affection alive in his face.

'But his kindness is the thing I most remember about him. He was kind to my mother, my sisters and me. I believe he loved us. And although his other family refused to acknowledge us, and that hurt and disappointed him, he also understood their hurt and jealousy, and he did what he could to mitigate it. He never said harsh words about them, ever, in my hearing.'

'I imagine that must've been some pretty difficult terrain for him to negotiate.'

'*Si.* And yet he refused to allow them to browbeat him. He refused to turn his back on us, even though it would've made for far more harmony in his life. He did what he thought was right.'

Lorenzo sounded like a truly good man.

'He was good to the people who worked for him too—helped out on the sly when they were sick—made sure they saw doctors, had enough food…whatever they needed. It made them very loyal to him.'

'What did he do for a living?'

'He owned vineyards. Mostly in the Piedmont region, though he had several in Lombardy too. Riposo was an anomaly—the only vineyard he owned in Tuscany.'

Just as Dante and his family had been an anomaly. And by giving this one to Dante's family, Lorenzo had been able to provide them with a home far away from the rest of his family. He'd been able to shield them from the worst of the resentment and animosity. 'He sounds like a wonderful man. I think what you're doing here is wonderful, Dante.'

He straightened. 'Thank you.'

He said the words so gravely they pierced her heart. She leaned towards him. 'And I promise I'll help you make a success of Lorenzo's in every way I can.'

He leaned towards her too. 'You have already promised to give me your best work.'

'But now I promise you my best work from my heart and not because you're paying me.'

He sagged as if her words had punched the breath from his body. 'I do not know what to say.'

She waved that away, reminded herself to channel some chilled holiday attitude. 'It's no biggie.'

His brows shot up. 'It is indeed a *biggie*, as you put it.'

First thing on the Help Make Lorenzo's a Success agenda was getting Dante to somehow loosen the control freak grip he had on every area of the restaurant's day-to-day running and allow the staff to do their jobs.

He frowned. 'Now you do not say anything. This is not usual. I do not trust it.'

She barked out a laugh. 'Okay, okay, it's just…'

'Yes?'

He leaned towards her again and his lemon, sage and sunshine scent drifted all around, making her far too aware of him. Instead of fixing on those tempting lips or mesmerising eyes, she stared down at the bar and made circles in the condensation her wineglass had left behind.

He reached out and closed his hand over hers. 'I wish you to be candid with me, Frankie. I promise no more temper tantrums.'

She found herself turning her hand up to entwine with his. It was meant to be a sign of solidarity and friendship. And initially it was exactly that. They smiled at each other as if that was innate and understood.

But then something flared. Something delicious and dangerous. Something that had no place in their relationship and they both snatched their hands back.

Frankie gulped a mouthful of wine. It shouldn't be gulped, gulping it was a sin, but she needed something to burn sense back into her. 'You agreed that you've lost perspective where the restaurant is concerned, and it's easy to see why. Lorenzo meant so much to you, and you want to create a fitting tribute to the man you loved and respected. But your grandfather would want you to do this with a joyful heart, wouldn't he? He wouldn't want it causing you so much stress and heartache.'

He stared at her as if he'd not considered such a thing.

'I think you ought to be having fun and feeling joy at what you're doing. I know there's the inevitable stress and worry as well, but it shouldn't be negating the excitement.'

He didn't say anything.

She shifted on her seat. 'Maybe you don't agree with me and, obviously, that's fine too. I just… You wanted me to tell you what was on my mind.'

'I am not angry at what you have said.'

She let out a breath.

'You have given me a different perspective, which I appreciate.'

He didn't look appreciative.

'This attitude of mine, it is not one that is complimentary to my grandfather. You are right. He would want me to enjoy this process. Instead, I am treating it like a mountain I must climb or an obligation I need to see through to completion. I must do better.'

And just like that he'd gone and put even more pressure on himself. It was all Frankie could do not to drop her head to her arms. Instead, she asked a question she'd been burning to ask from the get-to. '*Are* you a good chef?'

He nodded. 'It is my passion. I learned from a very good chef in the village when we first moved here. He took me under his wing. I learned much. In my leisure time I cook to relax. When I can spare the time, I hire masters to teach me new techniques and dishes.'

She stared at him, recognised the sudden fire in his eyes, and her mouth went dry. 'It makes you come alive, *feel* alive, when you're cooking?'

'*Si*, it is the best feeling in the world.'

Her heart thumped. She used to feel like that about medicine. She wished she could get it back. She wished—

She broke off with a frown. 'If you love cooking so much, why aren't you doing that instead of whatever it is you normally do?'

'Which would be running a multimillion-dollar construction business.'

Okay, so he really was super successful.

'I have a talent for business too.'

She reached across and poked him in the chest. 'Talent and passion are not the same thing. Which do you love more? If you were king of the world, and could choose to do anything, what would you choose?'

Dante's chest burned at Frankie's question. No one had ever asked him what he wanted before. His throat ached as he allowed himself to consider it.

Cooking filled his soul, made him feel complete in a way nothing else did, but not everyone was lucky enough to follow their dreams. Not everyone wanted to fritter away their life savings—*and their grandmother's*—on a life made up of holidays, ukuleles and grape picking.

'I have responsibilities, Frankie. Not everyone has the luxury of being able to follow their passions.'

The way she slid back in her seat away from him, made him realise how pointed that had sounded—the words shot at her as if from a gun.

Why? Because she didn't have the same responsibilities that he did? That wasn't fair. 'I greatly enjoy my business success,' he managed in a milder tone. 'I like what I have achieved.' It might not be his passion, but it didn't make those words any less true. 'What is your passion?'

She stared down into her wine. 'I don't know. I mean I thought I knew, once, but now I'm not so sure.' She shrugged, sent him a small smile. 'That's why I'm here in Tuscany.'

He had no right to judge her *or* to resent her freedom. Especially when she had just told him she would do everything she could to help him make Lorenzo's a success. When all she really wanted was a summer free of complications.

She was the only person so far brave enough to tell him where she thought he was going wrong, and to offer suggestions for how he could do better. He should be cherishing her, not rebuking her.

He straightened. He should be helping her. 'How is it you plan to discover your passion?'

'That's what this summer is all about—lots of

relaxing in the sun, lots of time to ponder the future while noodling about doing things I enjoy, with no responsibilities impinging on my time. I'm hoping three months of that will help me consider the future with a clearer eye.'

Except now it wasn't going to be such a carefree time, was it? He'd bullied her into being maître d' and had somehow made her feel invested in Lorenzo's success. He opened his mouth to tell her that he would find another maître d'' immediately, but closed it again. He wasn't prepared to let her go. His instinct—the business instinct that rarely let him down—told him that Frankie had what it took, that indefinable X factor, that would help him make Lorenzo's a success.

His hands clenched and unclenched. He *had* to do Lorenzo proud. And if Lorenzo were watching from above—if such things were possible— he did not want his beloved grandfather to think that this restaurant was in any way a chore or burden. It was a joy.

At least, it *would* be a joy once it was a success.

'Maybe I don't have a passion. Maybe there are lots of things I like, but no one single thing that's a passion.'

'*Dio*, everyone has a passion!'

He wished the words back the moment they left him. As if aware of an altogether different kind of passion, her gaze lowered to his lips and her blue eyes darkened to sapphire.

He had not meant *that* kind of passion. He ground his teeth together. This heat circling through his veins, and hers if he were reading her correctly, had to be ignored.

Forcing steel to his backbone, he straightened. 'I apologise if working at Lorenzo's is playing havoc with your plans.'

She snapped away as if his words had released her from a spell. Reaching up, she pulled her hair into a makeshift ponytail, not meeting his eyes. 'Stop wracking yourself with guilt and feeling responsible for *all the things*, Dante. It wasn't part of the plan, but then I realised not being wedded to any particular plan is what this summer should be about. I've simply decided to go with the flow. Maybe this job comes with more responsibility than I'd envisaged, but it's only for a month.'

Would a month be long enough, though? He'd barely started making enquiries about a suitable chef. What if he—?

No. He could not ask more of her. 'You do me a great favour and I appreciate it. I do not want you thinking otherwise.'

She let her hair fall back down around her shoulders. 'You *are* paying me,' she pointed out.

She was worth twice the money. 'Maybe there will be something I can do for you in return.' He would like to help her find a passion that would make her soul sing.

Those irrepressible eyes started to dance. 'Do

you mean that? If so, then something immediately comes to mind.'

Unfortunately, several things came to his mind too, but none of them were fit to utter in polite company. All of them involved spreading her out on a large bed and—

Dio!

He rolled his shoulders, not meeting her eyes. 'Let me guess, it involves me playing a ukulele.'

A laugh gurgled out of her and she started humming 'You Are My Sunshine', and he couldn't explain why, but he found himself torn between laughter and exasperation.

'No, this is something much closer to home— *your* home, Dante. Come grape picking with me.'

He found himself placing a hand on his heart. 'The grapes aren't ready yet. In a few weeks' time, before you leave Riposo, Frankie, I will take you grape picking.'

On Lorenzo's opening night, Dante paced the length of the kitchen, past the long preparation bench, past the ovens and hot plates and then around the servery and back again. He was aware of the looks exchanged by his kitchen staff, of the way they tensed and fidgeted, but could do nothing to temper the tension that coiled him up tight—tension that felt strangely like panic.

This had been a bad idea. He should've delayed

the opening when he'd discovered Eleanora's duplicity.

And allowed the general public to suspect Lorenzo's somehow lacking?

He slammed to a halt. *Never!* This was the lesser of two evils. But he should have moved heaven and earth to find a new chef.

In a week?

He ground his teeth together. He needed to find a chef with vision, a chef he could trust, a chef Lorenzo's deserved. Not someone who was simply available.

Stretching his neck first to the left and then to the right, he set to pacing again. He had the talent to fill in as head chef. He'd been offered positions in some of the finest restaurants in Italy. He knew food in the same way a musician knew the right notes to play on a piano, or the way an accomplished author knew what words to use to paint a vivid picture in a reader's mind. He knew what ingredients to put together to create a meal that would be long remembered in a diner's mind.

It was just…

He ought to be out there overseeing *everything*!

Frankie chose that moment to come waltzing into the kitchen, her eyes bright, a smile curving those luscious lips, everything about her exuding enthusiasm…and that indefinable something that had things inside of him shifting, tightening, *wanting*.

He tried to pinpoint exactly what it was she made him want. Because whatever she currently radiated, it wasn't sexual. He couldn't deny his stirring of sexual desire in reaction to just seeing her, but this was something different, something *more*.

Her gaze fixed on him, her eyes narrowed, and then she laughed. 'Oh, Dante, you really do have the soul of a chef, even if you manage to keep it trapped behind your cool-as-a-cucumber business demeanour most of the time.'

Behind him he was aware of his kitchen staff tensing even further. He glared at her.

'I mean look at you—all volatile and tempestuous.' She huffed out another laugh. 'You have your poor staff shaking in their boots.'

'Nonsense!' he snapped. 'I am not this mythical, unreasonable, tyrannical boss you wish to make me out to be.'

Her eyes danced. 'I'm sure they'll be glad to hear it.'

Was she deliberately trying to rile him?

'Okay, Dante, listen to me. All *you* need to focus on tonight is creating beautiful dishes to send out to our beautiful diners.'

But he wanted—*needed*—to know how the diners were reacting—

'You're the boss in here, but out there *I'm* the boss.'

He blinked.

She folded her arms and stuck her nose in the air. 'And I forbid you from coming out into the dining room.'

He clenched his hands so hard he started to shake. '*You* forbid *me*? You forget—'

'I won't have you frightening my diners.'

He gaped at her.

She moved in a step closer and her eyes gentled. 'I'm very good at my job, Dante. You know this. It's why you hired me.'

He closed his eyes and dragged in air scented with amber and carnations.

'You've hired the best waitstaff I've ever worked with.'

What she said was true. He *had* hired the best.

'My waitstaff and I are going to provide the best service tonight's diners have experienced in a long time. But good service will only take us so far. What's really going to put Lorenzo's on the map and make the dining experience extraordinary is the food, and you've put together a magnificent menu.'

He opened his eyes. 'This is a menu that cannot be beaten.' He planted his feet. 'I have hired the very best kitchen staff too.'

At his words, his staff all straightened.

'It is just this waiting for our first orders is hard.'

'Well, we'll be busy enough before you know it. Now, do I have your word that you'll focus on the food, rather than peering out the door every two minutes and checking on everything and upsetting everyone? Will you leave me to focus on the service?'

He knew she was right, but it felt precariously like giving control to someone else, and that was not something that came easily to him.

She stepped closer. 'You need to trust your staff,' she said softly. 'You know we're the best. Between us all, we can and will wow tonight's diners.'

He found his lips curving into an unexpected smile. Perhaps it was the picture her words created in his mind. Perhaps it was the confidence that shone from her eyes. 'How is it you put it, Frankie? You have yourself a deal.'

She laughed and he felt as if he'd done something magical.

She glanced at his kitchen staff. 'We're going to do Dante's late grandfather, Lorenzo, proud tonight, everyone. He was a very good man who made a big difference in a lot of people's lives. Our world would be a much better place if there were more people like Lorenzo in it.'

Her words made his eyes burn and his throat thicken.

'Also, for those who have the time to stay, we'll be having prosecco and nibbles in the dining room afterwards to celebrate tonight's opening, as a thank-you for giving your finest efforts.'

Dio. This was an excellent idea. Why had he not thought of it himself?

She rubbed her hands together and did a funny little happy dance on the spot. 'It's almost time for the doors to open. C'mon, Dante, test me on my knowledge. Give me a meal I need to pair with a good wine.'

'Veal scallopine.'

Her eyes widened in outrage. 'That's not on the menu!'

He folded his arms and tapped a foot, raising what he hoped was an infuriating eyebrow. He'd taught her reds on Thursday. She'd discovered a love of Brunello.

She tossed her head. 'I would suggest a Pinot Noir. It would give the palate a nice clean finish.'

'You are getting very good.'

'I keep telling you that.'

She turned on her heel and exited the room, and he realised she'd changed the entire dynamic in the kitchen. She had soothed the fear that had him in its grip. It was still there, but it no longer overshadowed his excitement or determination.

How had she done that? 'A most extraordinary woman,' he murmured.

Carlo, his second-in-command, nodded in hearty agreement.

He clapped his hands, that determination crystallising inside him. 'Very well, everyone, take your stations. Don't forget, if there is anything that you are unsure about, come and check with me. I will not bite off your head. And if I happen to yell at anyone, or yell in general, it is my excitement not because I am angry…and I will apologise at the end of the evening.'

Before they knew it, orders began pouring in, and the kitchen became a frenzy of activity. Dante found himself grinning and grimacing and feeling more alive than he had in an age. At one point he'd started absentmindedly humming 'You Are My Sunshine'. When he momentarily took stock, after sending one dish out into the dining room and before starting on the next, he realised his entire kitchen hummed the tune with him. It felt somehow right.

Dante glanced up from the desk in his office bright and early Monday morning when he heard Frankie calling out his name from the corridor outside. What on earth was she doing up so early? Her efforts over the last two nights definitely deserved a sleep in this morning. His opening weekend had gone better than he could've hoped, and that was in large part due to her. The next few days were hers to do with as she pleased. He'd told her as much last night when they'd closed up.

He rose and rounded his desk as she burst in brandishing a newspaper. 'Lorenzo's has received the most wonderful write-up, Dante! *Glowing!*'

Someone from the press had been here? 'Listen! Listen!' She bounced on the spot.

'If the opening weekend is anything to go by, Lorenzo's has proved itself to be the place to dine this summer. In a region known for its fine wines and fine dining, Lorenzo's is making a mark. As welcoming and charming as both the setting and the service were—and I assure you both exceeded expectations— it was the food that was the star of the evening. Lorenzo's boasts an innovative menu with new twists on Italian classics that had this foodie's heart beating faster. I have one word to describe it: *divine*. My meal was one of the best I have had in a long time. And, in a twist all its own, the chef proved to be none other than homegrown boy made good, successful businessmen Dante Alberici. I urge you to put Lorenzo's on your must-try list this summer. You will not be disappointed.'

Dante stared at Frankie in open-mouthed awe. She continued to dance on the spot, and then she flung her arms around him. 'You did it, Dante! You did it!'

Sensation flooded him as their bodies met in a full-length embrace. He had not been expecting an armful of warm woman. Especially not one as vibrant and full of life as Frankie. Especially not one that in the space of a heartbeat, fired his blood with a heat that threatened to turn into an inferno. His hand went around her waist and he closed his eyes to inhale her scent. To imprint the feel of her on his brain.

She leaned back to stare up him, those generous lips in a wide smile. 'Lorenzo's is on its way to being the best restaurant in all of Tuscany!'

And then, as if suddenly aware of the direction of his thoughts, as if the heat in his veins infected her too, her breath hitched and her gaze lowered to his mouth. Blue eyes darkened to the colour of sparkling sapphires, and her tongue flicked out to moisten plump lips, and every nerve ending he had flared and burned.

CHAPTER FIVE

FRANKIE FELL INTO the swirling heat of Dante's eyes, not ever wanting to leave the exciting warmth of his arms. As if in total agreement, his fingers dug into the flesh of her hips, and the urgency of it made her gasp. A fierce and intense wildness swept through her, had her gripping his arms to stay upright.

The muscles beneath her fingers flexed and she could've groaned out loud at the strength and potency pulsing from him. Dante was pure masculine power and beauty and she wanted to lose herself in him. Thoughtlessly, mindlessly. Completely.

One large hand lifted to push her hair from her face. 'Like silk,' he murmured, brushing the backs of his fingers along her cheek. Her skin tingled and she arched into his touch, silently begging for more. More touching, more whispering, more everything.

Oh, this was a bad idea. A bad, bad idea.

'Frankie.' Her name sounded like a caress and a curse, both at the same time. And she understood it. It was as if her name had been dragged from the depths of him without his volition. This feeling building between them, it had taken him as off guard as her, and a man like Dante liked to be in control.

And she threatened that control. *Her.*

In that moment she didn't care if this was a bad idea or not. The fact she was shaking him to his foundations in the same way he did her shattered her restraint, filling her with satisfaction and joy. It made her bold; it made her soar.

His thumb brushed across her lower lip, pulling and dragging, building a need deep inside her that she'd never known before. Everything throbbed. She touched her tongue to his thumb, gently bit down on it, her eyes not leaving his.

She could reach up and drag his head down to hers, kiss him with all the fire building inside her, find relief and release in that mouth and all it could offer her.

Or she could do what he was doing now. Tantalise and tease, build the expectation until neither one of them could bear it.

Moving her hands to his chest, she tentatively explored the muscled contours hidden beneath his immaculately pressed business shirt. Slowly, deliberately, thoroughly. He sucked in a breath and tensed beneath her touch, those dark eyes flaring with hunger. Oh, how she wanted to see him ruffled and undone!

'This is madness,' he murmured. But he didn't move away. Instead, he wound his hand around her hair, pulled it back until her neck was exposed and he leaned down to graze the delicate skin there with his teeth. She couldn't contain her cry, couldn't prevent her hips from pressing against his where his erection throbbed against her. She wanted to wrap her entire body around his, guide him inside her and—

A low throaty moan sounded in the air. Hers? His arm tightened about her waist as if aware her legs were in danger of giving away.

He swore, but it sounded like a caress. *'Sei una tentatrice.'*

You are a temptress.

Nobody had ever called her a temptress before.

'Puzzi di paradiso.'

You smell like heaven.

His words built more heat, words whispering against her throat as he pressed hot drugging kisses there. This was divine madness and she couldn't get enough.

With palms and fingers, she teased flat male nipples into hard pointed arousal. 'You are perfection,' she murmured. She wanted to make him feel as beautiful and wanted as he did her.

A growl sounded from his throat, vibrating through her. Teeth closed around her earlobe and tugged gently. A tremor shook her entire body. Her breathing became jagged. Seizing her hips in firm hands, he pulled her more fully against him, and at the feel of him pressing at the very centre of her where she most wanted him, stars burst behind her eyelids.

They weren't even naked yet! He hadn't dipped his fingers beneath the hem of her T-shirt, she'd not pulled his shirt from the waistband of his beautifully tailored trousers, and yet she'd never felt more on fire in her life.

Her fingers immediately moved down that taut stomach to tug his shirt free.

'If I kiss you, Frankie, I do not think I will want to stop.'

He was asking her if this was what she wanted. He was asking her permission to continue.

Of course she wanted him to continue! If he should stop now, she might die. And yet her fingers stilled at his words.

And what of tomorrow? some inner voice demanded. *What of an hour from now when this is over?*

Shut up! she wanted to shout.

He dragged in a breath, rested his forehead against hers. 'You hesitate.'

And then he put her away from him and she missed the warmth and the magic, and had to reach out a hand to the desk to find her balance. Her body itched and burned, demanding more of his drugging kisses, more of his touch. She burned for release and pleasure—

At what cost?

He still stood near, as if waiting for her to reach out for him, but she snapped away from him so quickly he had to grab her arm and right her as she started to fall over the chair behind. As soon as she had her balance again, he moved back behind his desk.

'Oh, God, Dante, I'm sorry. I've gone and made things weird between us again. I just meant that hug to be a congratulations for Lorenzo's successful opening weekend. I didn't mean—'

She wanted to stamp a foot. She was seriously bad at the whole relaxed, carefree thing. But, worse than that, she was losing sight of why she was here, losing sight of what she owed her grandmother—wasting this opportunity that had been given to her.

She was a *bad* granddaughter. She was a *bad* daughter. She glanced at Dante. She was a bad person.

He shook his head. 'That was not your fault. I lost my head in the moment and—' lips twisted in self-disgust '—it was unforgivable. I apologise, Frankie. I'm a grown man, not some hormone-riddled youth. I should've known better and—'

'Stop it!' She fell down into the chair, not sure her trembling legs would keep her upright a moment longer. 'I'm not going to toss you for the blame. If we're being honest and adult—' two things she very much needed to be this summer '—we're both to blame.'

He sat too, rubbed a hand over his face. 'There is a heat that exists between us. These things have no rhyme or reason. They just are. But we are not animals.'

'We can resist it if we choose.'

'We must.' He thrust out his jaw. 'You are my employee.'

She remembered what he thought of her and some devil made her say. 'Only temporarily.'

His nostrils flared; on the desk his hands clenched. 'You toy with me?'

Good Lord, what was she thinking? Swallowing, she shook her head. 'I'm sorry. I know you think me some careless flibbertigibbet—'

'This word, I do not know.'

'An irresponsible person.'

'Ah.' He leaned back.

'But I don't usually jump into a sexual relationship without giving it at least some thought first. That was why I hesitated. Things moved far more quickly than I expected them to, than I realised they had. I lost my head.' Her heart thumped. 'And if you hadn't slowed us down to ask the question, my head may have remained lost.'

They'd have made love and…

Her body dissolved at the thought. She did what she could to ignore the itching and prickling and yearning.

'And afterwards you would have regretted that?'

Would she? She dragged her hands through her hair. 'I don't know.'

Yes, you do.

His lips thinned. 'This is not what your face tells me.'

Dammit! How could he read her so easily? 'Okay, yes, I'd have regretted it. Not because I don't like you, because I like you just fine.'

He blinked.

'And not because I don't think it would've been pleasurable, because all the indications tell me it would be off the charts.'

'Off the charts? This is a good thing?'

It was a very good thing. Not that she needed to stress that any further. Or to even think about it. 'When did you learn English, Dante?' She folded her arms. Everything still felt shaky and needy and she wished she could just make it stop.

'Not until I was twelve.'

When Lorenzo had swept in to provide him with a home and a good education. It explained why he didn't recognise some of the more esoteric expressions she used.

'When did you learn Italian?' he asked in turn.

'I'm not completely fluent but my mother and grandmother taught me from the cradle. When I was growing up, on Mondays and Tuesdays we spoke Italian. The rest of the time we spoke English.' She shrugged. 'Or a mix.'

'That sounds nice.' Dark eyes throbbed into hers. 'So tell me why you'd have regretted making love?'

Why did he want to know? Did he hope to overcome her objections? The thought had heat circling in her bloodstream again, had her fingers clenching together in an effort to counter the heat and need.

'And then I will tell you why I would've regretted it, even though I'd have not stopped if you hadn't hesitated. It is my belief that if we are aware of the other person's reasons, we can doubly arm ourselves against future temptation.'

That made sense. Closing her eyes, she pulled in a breath. 'This summer is important to me. I have some big decisions to make. I don't want a man distracting me from making those decisions.' She hesitated. 'Or influencing them.'

She needed to work out the life *she* wanted. Not the life someone else dreamed for her.

'That sounds remarkably sensible.'

She laughed. She couldn't help it. It still delighted her that he thought her a free spirit. 'I guess it comes to all of us, eventually.' Shuffling upright, she clapped. 'Your turn.'

The pulse at his jaw jerked as if he clenched it too hard. It made her tired just watching it.

'First of all, you are in my employ. There is a power dynamic there that is problematic. I would not want a sexual relationship to threaten an important working relationship.'

The way he said the words made her realise that he wasn't worried so much about her feelings being exploited. He was worried about alienating her or distressing her in some way and her cutting short her tenure as his maître d' in a huff. Which meant he thought the power in their relationship rested with her.

And that was food for thought. But he was also right, she realised. She didn't need his money. She could find work elsewhere easily enough. She could get into Bertha whenever she liked and drive off into the sunset.

'In addition to that, like you, I do not want the distraction of a romance at this current moment in time. I want to exclusively focus on Lorenzo's.' He gestured to the newspaper lying on his desk. 'And we have started well. I would not want to do anything to jeopardise that.'

Dark eyes pinned her to the spot. 'Lorenzo the man, my grandfather, deserves my finest efforts. I want to do this for him—to honour him, to show my gratitude and my love for him.'

She understood that need in her bones. After all, if it wasn't for her grandmother she'd still be nose to the grindstone and living other people's dreams. In their different ways, they both wanted to pay homage to their grandparent.

'To become distracted with a frivolous affair...
It feels disrespectful.'

Wow. Okay. She'd have not put it as strongly as
that. Dante really needed to chill out.

Not with you.

She shot to her feet. 'Right. Well. It's good to
know where each of us stands. We have far more
important things to focus on this summer.'

'*Si.*'

'We agree to keep our relationship strictly professional.'

'*Si.* As you say—we have a deal.'

She nodded, but neither one of them offered
to shake on it. From now on, there'd be as little
touching as possible.

On Thursday night, they had a full house. The restaurant hummed with anticipation and a kind of
low-key conviviality that straddled a perfect line
between high spirits and relaxation. And Frankie
was somehow the embodiment of it all. Dante did
his best *not* to notice Frankie, however.

He started when a crash sounded from the dining room—*again*—breaking crockery shattering the warm hum. He turned and glared at the
kitchen doors. That was the third time tonight.
And each time it had sent a ripple of discord
through the dining room's convivial atmosphere,
threatening to overshadow the harmony.

A moment later, Frankie appeared and requested another *pollo alla cacciatore* and *ragu toscano* as fast as possible. One glance at her and he recalled that blistering near kiss in his office on Monday, and it made him burn with barely repressed need, which did nothing to improve his temper. Doing his best to ignore it, he fired instructions to his under chefs and whipped up a complimentary appetiser for her to take out to the couple whose dinner had obviously ended up on the dining room floor.

'Frankie—'

'It's under control, Dante, I promise.'

He knew he must have a face like thunder, and while to all appearances Frankie appeared as breezy and buoyant as ever, he sensed chagrin burning just beneath the surface. A quick glance around the kitchen, though, and he realised nobody else sensed it. Lorenzo's diners would not sense it either. Frankie would go out there and make all calm again.

But what if it happened a fourth time. He couldn't—

She lifted the appetisers, balancing both plates effortlessly on one arm. 'I'm afraid our new waitress isn't feeling well. I've sent her home.'

All of that havoc had been caused by one waitress?

'We'll have a small dry-cleaning bill, but it's nothing that can't be fixed.' She nodded at the complimentary appetisers and sent him a smile.

'And with these and a complimentary glass of Riposo's award-winning prosecco, our diners may even think the accident a blessing.'

And then she was gone and he knew grilling her for details now would be counterproductive. They were down a waitress and the dining room staff were going to be busy and Frankie would be picking up the slack. They'd have a debrief at the end of the night like they had last Saturday and Sunday nights.

He did what he could to put the incidents from his mind, to cook with a happy and grateful heart. He had only a short time to enjoy this stint as a head chef. He would take a leaf from Frankie's book and make the most of it. For his grandfather's sake, he would not cook with an anxious, unhappy heart. He would cook with gladness and appreciation.

'Tell me why you were so unhappy tonight?' Dante demanded later that evening when the last of the staff had said their farewells.

Frankie spun around, eyes wide. She opened her mouth and then closed it. Folding her arms, she stuck out a hip. 'That waitress…'

'Yes?' He waited. 'Are you keeping something from me?' he demanded when she hesitated. 'I am not a child that needs protecting. Nor am I an unreasonable tyrant from whom the staff need protecting. You will tell me at once what this thing is!'

Her lips twitched. 'Not a tyrant, huh?'

He could feel his nose wrinkle.

'You really should take better care of your blood pressure, or you'll blow a blood vessel.'

His lips twisted too.

'I'm not keeping anything from you, Dante. I'm trying to find the words to give voice to something I'm not even sure of, that's all.'

Why did he always jump to the wrong conclusion where Frankie was concerned? He might think her a *flibbertigibbet*, as she put it, but she hadn't been anything other than professional in his dining room. 'I apologise,' he said stiffly. 'Come,' he gestured to the bar, 'let us have a drink. What would you like?'

Frankie had pronounced the bar area as "small, but perfectly formed" when she'd first seen it. Four bar stools ran the length of the bar and four bucket seats arranged around a low table sat beside the hearth, which they would light in autumn when the weather turned cooler.

She settled into one of the bucket seats with a sigh. 'Surprise me.'

Remorse prickled through him. She'd been on her feet all evening. She'd not had a single break. Once she'd sent that waitress home, the rest of the evening had been smooth and trouble free. She didn't deserve his bellowing and bellyaching.

Seizing a bottle of red, he took her hand and tugged her to her feet and towed her into the kitchen. He then went back into the dining room and carried in a table and two chairs and seated her at one. 'What would you like to eat?'

Her eyes widened. 'You don't need to cook for me.'

'I would like to.' He meant it. 'I love to cook. You know this of me.'

'Are you going to join me?'

'*Si.*' If it meant that she would eat too.

She chewed on her bottom lip. 'What I want isn't on the menu.'

His mind immediately slipped to tangled sheets, hot bodies and entwined limbs and his mind blanked.

As if suddenly realising how her words could be interpreted, she coughed and turned an alarming shade of scarlet. 'An omelette,' she croaked out. 'I would like an omelette.'

He dragged his mind back to food. *And only food.* 'You ask me for this because it is simple and you don't want to put me to any trouble.'

'I ask for it because it's light and will be kind to my digestion. In another hour, I hope to be asleep.'

In her silly, lovely camper van that she called Bertha. He refused to imagine himself tucked into that cosy bed beside her. 'An omelette with ham, mushrooms and shallots?'

'Perfect.'

A short while later he set the omelettes to the table, poured them both a glass of wine.

She touched her glass to his and nodded at her plate. 'Thank you for this.'

'My pleasure.'

They both sipped, and her lids fluttered in appreciation. 'This is lovely.'

He didn't quiz her on what it was. He simply wanted her to enjoy it. 'Try your omelette.'

She lifted a forkful of omelette to her mouth and ate it. Her eyes closed and an expression of bliss raced across her face. 'How do you do that? How can you take a few ingredients and create something so wonderful?'

She forked more of the omelette into her mouth, and he smiled as she groaned her appreciation. *Dio!* She loved what he had cooked. The knowledge warmed him all the way through. He didn't try questioning her again about the events of the evening. He merely wanted her to enjoy her food and wine, and the peace and quiet. She'd earned it.

She eventually wiped her plate clean with the slice of sourdough he'd placed on the side of her plate, set her knife and fork neatly together and blotted her mouth with a napkin. He stared at that empty plate. She must've been starving! He should've taken better care of her. 'Can I get you more toast? Or perhaps you would like a dessert? A slice of *zuccotto*, perhaps, or—'

'I couldn't eat another thing, Dante. I ate more than I should've anyway, but it was too delicious and I couldn't stop.'

Was she telling him the truth? This woman, she was sometimes too carelessly happy-go-lucky. Was she skipping meals? Was she looking after herself?

'That's the best omelette I've ever eaten.'

She made him feel like a maestro. 'I am pleased you enjoyed it. I am sorry you did not get your break this evening.'

'I had a very hearty sandwich before my shift, full of cheese and cured meats and salad. It's wise in this business to be prepared for all eventualities, like having to miss one's break.'

He'd bet she'd made sure all of her waitstaff had their breaks, though.

'So about Carla, the waitress...'

His attention snapped back.

'She has me puzzled. Her qualifications were excellent.'

They'd hired her only this afternoon. 'One of the waitstaff had called in sick, and it had felt like serendipity when this new waitress had presented herself in person with a view to leaving her résumé in case Lorenzo's planned to hire more waitstaff in the future. 'Si. She appeared personable and competent in her interview.'

Frankie nodded.

'But?' he prodded.

Clear blue eyes met his and without warning his heart started to pound. Clenching his hands, he tried to focus on what Frankie was trying to say, rather than the debilitating way his body ached and craved her. Frankie glanced at his fists, frowned, and then glanced up into his face before her gaze darted away again. She swallowed, and her fingers started to drum against her wineglass. Beneath the table her foot jigged. She was as aware of him as he was of her and it took all his strength to remain where he was.

'Accidents happened.' The words left her like bullets.

'Yes,' he bit out, vexed with himself. He needed to be more careful, more guarded.

'Carla...'

With a start, he realised she referred to the waitress, not what had happened between him and her on Monday morning. He forced himself back into straight lines. 'It is inevitable. Accidents will sometimes happen in both the dining room and the kitchen.' He tapped a finger against his mouth. 'But three in one night?'

'And all caused by the same person.'

Something in her tone had his senses sharpening. 'What are you saying?'

'I don't really know. I'd understand her being nervous on the first night, but she has had a lot of experience. One accident I could understand, but three...'

He leaned towards her, watching her face carefully.

'She didn't mention not feeling well, and she

didn't look unwell.' Her gaze darted to his. 'It's something I pay attention to because we work with food, and it's not good practise to allow sick staff to work. Our diners deserve better.'

He tried to hide his surprise at her attention to detail. There was so much he didn't know about running a restaurant. Cooking—yes. But as for the rest of it… He understood in that moment why she hadn't wanted the maître d' role, and a dark grey mist rolled through his soul. It hadn't been fair of him to force her hand and make her take the job.

'And something Brianna said to me—she collided with Carla, which was incident number two.'

'What did she say?'

'That she didn't see Carla until the incident happened. That Carla had remained out of her line of sight, wasn't even in her peripheral vision until the very last minute.' Her frown deepened. 'When you're experienced—' those lovely eyes rolled '—when there's a collision or two lurking in your past, you learn to become hyperaware of the people around you.'

The way she said it made him think a couple such incidents rested in her past too.

'Normally you see something from the corner of your eye. And even if you can't avoid an accident, you can often mitigate it, but Brianna said it was as if Carla had snuck up on her.'

He stiffened. 'Did she accuse Carla of doing so deliberately?'

'Oh, no, it was nothing like that. More a throw-away comment.' Her lips pursed. 'But Carla had no business being on that side of the restaurant.'

'She may have just lost her bearings.'

'Yes.'

She didn't sound convinced. 'Are you accusing her of deliberately staging those accidents?'

She shook her head, frowning. 'Something feels off, that's all. I just can't put my finger on it. I asked her to wait for me in my office before she left so we could have a brief chat before she went home.'

He'd given Frankie the small office beside his. She might only be temporary, but she needed access to staff files and email while she was maître d'.

'I only kept her waiting five minutes while I settled things in the dining room, but when I got to my office, she wasn't there.'

'Why not?'

'I've no idea as she didn't answer her phone either.'

She stared at him with pursed lips, and he straightened. 'What?'

'You hadn't met her before, had you?'

'I do not believe so.'

'She's not a scorned woman from your past?'

'Absolutely not!'

'Are there any scorned women in your past who would want to do you a mischief?'

He went cold. 'That is…'

'Outrageous? None of my business? Ridiculous?' she supplied for him. 'I couldn't agree more. It's just, like I said, something about this doesn't feel right.'

His mind raced. She didn't think the events of this evening as accidental. Was there someone in his past who bore him a grudge? He dragged a hand down his face. He worked in the cutthroat world of big business. There would be many who'd like to see him humbled.

Frankie didn't have any evidence, though, only a gut feeling.

And experience, a voice whispered. He nodded. He needed to be on his guard from now on and keep his eyes and ears open. 'Did you dismiss her?'

Startled blue eyes met his. 'Of course not. I wouldn't do such a thing without consulting you first.'

That wasn't necessary. He trusted her. The realisation made him blink.

'And it's not reasonable to fire someone just because they've had one bad night. But, Dante, I'm going with my instincts on this one and won't be rostering her on again. At least not until she contacts me and offers me an explanation.'

He nodded. '*Si*, I approve of this plan.'

The following morning, Dante read the emails that had just hit his inbox *three times* before exploding into a torrent of curses. The chair in the office next door scraped against the floor and a few seconds later Frankie appeared in his doorway.

She took one look at his face and her brows shot up. 'What's wrong?'

He stabbed a shaking finger at his computer screen and the offending emails, not trusting himself to speak. She moved across with a reassuring briskness to read them for herself—it was clear she could read Italian as well as she could speak it. Easing back, she cursed too. He couldn't explain why, but it made him want to laugh.

But then the import of those emails slammed into him again and he wanted to throw his head back and roar. His two main suppliers had just informed him that they wouldn't be able to supply him with the meat or poultry he'd ordered for the rest of the weekend, or the fruit and vegetables.

This… It was a disaster!

CHAPTER SIX

THINK, FRANKIE, THINK! Frankie wanted to find a solution and lower Dante's blood pressure *pronto*, help him bypass that prospective ulcer. Getting this worked up wasn't good for anyone. This man who was a self-proclaimed cucumber had no perspective when it came to Lorenzo's.

She knew what it was like to want to pay homage so badly it churned up your insides and robbed you of the ability to think straight or see clearly, though. 'They can't be the only suppliers.'

'Of course not, but look at the time! And I only source the *best* produce.'

And paid a pretty penny for it too, she'd bet.

'All that will be left now from the markets will be what others haven't deemed good enough, and those are not the standards for which I want Lorenzo's to be known.'

Her ears pricked. 'Quality is more important to you than price?'

'Yes.'

'And you're judging Lorenzo's success on the

quality of its food and the experience it provides rather than it making a lot of money quickly.'

'*Si.*'

'And you're a wealthy man.'

'Why does this matter?'

'Because it means you can source produce from pretty much anywhere in Italy and have it helicoptered in, if you're prepared to pay through the nose to make such a thing happen.'

He raced around the desk, seized her shoulders in firm fingers. 'You are a genius!'

She found herself lifted onto her tiptoes as warm, firm lips smacked to hers in an exuberant kiss that sent ribbons of heat snaking through her bloodstream and had her breath jamming in her throat.

Startled eyes the colour of espresso coffee met hers and he immediately released her, cleared his throat. 'I'm sorry. That… I should not have done it.'

She tried to shrug the moment off. 'It was the equivalent of my hug on Monday.' But need and want jostled inside her, demanding she *do* something.

Absolutely not!

'A spur of the moment exuberance,' he choked out.

They both swallowed and looked away. She swiped damp palms down the sides of her sundress and wished she didn't like the way he put a sentence together so much.

They glanced back at each other again. 'Don't go all smouldery and seductive on me,' she snapped.

'Then don't give me that big limpid gaze begging me to—'

'*Limpid?*' she spluttered. 'Where did you learn a word like that?'

'This I cannot remember, and it is unimportant. I am simply pointing out—'

'Suppliers!' She clapped her hands together, *hard*, wanting their minds back on the task at hand.

He rubbed a hand over his face, moved back behind his desk. 'As I was saying, you are a genius. It is the perfect solution.

'And one you'd have thought of yourself soon enough.' She pointed at him. 'Cool as a cucumber, remember?'

His lips pressed together, but he nodded. 'Thank you. I will start to organise this immediately.' He jabbed the intercom of his phone and barked orders into it.

'Do you need me to do anything?'

'No.' His gaze suddenly cleared. 'It is morning, Frankie. What are you doing working?'

She edged towards the door. 'I was just checking to make sure nobody had rung in sick for tonight. I'm done now.'

He waved a hand at the window. 'Go and enjoy the sun, play your ukulele, enjoy your leisure time.'

With a nod, she left. But her summer working holiday suddenly seemed small and frivolous. She couldn't help thinking that last night's incident with the waitress and today's supply issues were somehow linked.

Even if she was right, though, she had no proof. Three of Dante's assistants came rushing down the corridor towards his office. And now wasn't the right time to raise the topic with him. She pressed herself against the wall to let them pass, staring after them wistfully.

Stop being ridiculous. She had a valley to explore. And a mind to de-stress, so she could get it to a place where she could take stock and make the decisions she needed to.

The day darkened. What if she was no closer to knowing the answers at summer's end? What if this summer didn't achieve any of the desired outcomes her grandmother had hoped for? What if—?

Dragging in air into lungs threatening to cramp, she concentrated on her breathing. She had time. Lots of time. Panicking about it wouldn't help. Panicking about Lorenzo's wouldn't help either.

Dante would be fine. He had an army of staff at his fingertips. Both the man and the restaurant could function without her. Using them as a displacement activity was not the reason her grandmother had made this summer possible for her.

Go and do something fun.

'You are quiet,' Dante said as they finished up in the restaurant on Friday night. 'It is out of character.'

She didn't think it was. It was just out of character for the persona she'd adopted here at Riposo. Or was the persona she'd adopted at home the fake one? The thought had her swallowing.

'Is there something troubling you?'

She turned with hands on hips. 'Yes,' she said with sudden decision. She could be wrong, but if she wasn't…

He took her arm and led her to one of the bucket seats by the fire, took the one opposite and simply waited. She appreciated that about him—that he didn't rush or pressure her.

Pressing her hands together, she met his gaze. 'Do you think there's something going on—something iffy? First the waitress last night and then your suppliers this morning.'

His eyes throbbed. 'It's never wise to jump to conclusions.'

It wasn't an answer. 'I agree,' she said carefully. 'But nor is it wise to bury one's head in the sand.' She was proof positive of that.

'You think someone is sabotaging the restaurant?'

'I don't know. You use big name suppliers, right?'

He nodded.

'These are companies that have built a reputation based in part on their reliability.' She frowned. 'They do know who they're supplying, don't they?'

'Lorenzo's is a new customer.' One broad shoulder lifted. If there is a supply issue, they would perhaps prioritise their older customers first.'

That made her snort. 'They have to know that Lorenzo's and Dante Alberici are one and the same. Why would they let down someone with your clout? It makes no commercial sense.'

He remained silent.

She might not have any proof, but it would be foolhardy to ignore early warning signs of trouble. 'Dante, is there anyone who would want to hurt you?' Her mouth went dry at the thought.

He rubbed a hand over his face. When he pulled it away, he looked so exhausted her heart ached for him. It took all her strength to remain where she was, rather than to move across and hug him.

'It is something I have been pondering all day. I share your concerns that this could be more than a coincidence.' He let out a breath. 'Perhaps a business rival would wish me ill. There are companies who have lost contracts to me in the past. That kind of…disappointment can generate hostility. Maybe a disgruntled employee. It is inevitable, in a business the size of mine, that some people will feel aggrieved and resentful for any number of reasons.'

She grimaced. 'Has anyone tried to sabotage you in the past?'

Dark eyes met hers, and he gave the tiniest of nods. 'When I was first starting out and trying to attract investors.'

'Who?' she prompted when he remained silent.

'Lorenzo's legitimate family.'

Things inside her sagged.

'I never told him. But when I discovered the source of the trouble, I hit back hard and fast. They did not try such a thing again.'

She didn't ask what they'd done or what he'd done in retaliation.

'But Lorenzo is dead. They know he would not wish for them to interfere in my life or business. I think they would have too much respect for his wishes to do so.'

She hesitated. She didn't want to ask, but...

'Would your father wish you ill?'

His hands clenched. 'He has no right to wish me ill. It is I who has cause to be aggrieved with him!'

She held her hands up. 'I agree wholeheartedly. I'm just—'

'You are trying to help.' He subsided back into his seat. 'And I appreciate it.' He met her gaze, and nodded. 'I will start enquiries.'

She left it at that.

'Frankie, I know you keep assuring me you're well, but your grandfather is worried too.'

Her grandfather?

Frankie leaped up and paced a path around Bertha, phone pressed to her ear, the sun no longer warm on her face. Her mother was bringing out the big guns. Grandfather was a *cannon*-sized big gun.

'We don't want you doing something you'll later

regret. I know you would like to do your father proud, and we're proud of the path you've chosen, but—'

'There's more than one way to make someone proud,' she cut in, slamming to a halt. 'But it feels as if you'll only be proud of me if I go ahead and become a surgeon.'

'That's not true! But, Frankie, what of all your training and plans? You have such a bright future ahead of you.'

'What if I don't want that future?' She swallowed. 'What if it's making me miserable?'

There was a long pause.

'Or doesn't that matter to you?' she made herself ask, her eyes burning with tears she refused to shed.

'Frankie!'

She didn't know if it was shock or remonstrance in her mother's voice. 'I need some time, Mum. Can't you just please give it to me? I need to gain some perspective and gather my thoughts. Please don't ring me again.'

She turned the phone off and stared at the scene in front of her—grapevines under a summer sun—tried to drag its tranquillity and holiday vibe into her soul. *Happy-go-lucky and carefree*, she recited the words over and over in her mind.

Frankie started awake when someone thumped on the side of her van in the wee small hours of

Monday morning. She sat up in bed, trying to blink the sleep from her eyes.

'Frankie?'

Dante?

'Frankie, wake up! We're going to be late.'

What on earth...? The weekend was over. Lorenzo's had surpassed itself as usual—there'd been no more supply problems and no more waitstaff incidents—and she now had three well-earned days off.

Scooting down the bed, she slid open the door, stifling a yawn. 'Late for what?'

He stared at her and she was suddenly aware that she was wearing nothing but a tank top and a pair of sleep shorts. She fought the urge to seize the sheet and wrap it around her. What she was wearing was perfectly respectable. 'Late for what?' she repeated, trying to smooth her hair down.

'Grape picking.'

He'd promised to take her grape picking today. She grabbed her watch from the bench. 'It's two-thirty in the morning. The grape picking shift starts at seven, Dante, so—'

'For the Sangiovese and cabernet grapes, yes. But today we're picking the chardonnay grapes. They must be picked at the time they are freshest and before the heat of the sun has touched them.'

Was he serious? Night-time grape picking? Behind him, the seasonal workers' staff quarters were brightly lit and the sound of people getting ready reached her. As she shared the staff bathroom, and as the workers also liked to sit out in the warmth of the afternoon, she'd made friends with several of them. No doubt the bus from the village would arrive soon with the rest of the grape picking staff.

Night-time grape picking? That could be fun! Seizing her toiletry bag and a bundle of clothes, she hopped out of the van. 'I'll be ready in ten.'

She was ready in eight and doing her best not to question the anticipation rising through her. 'You did that on purpose,' she said when she walked back to Bertha and found him settled on one of her camp chairs as if he belonged there.

He spread his hands, suspiciously innocent. 'Did what?'

'Chose night-time grape picking instead of the daytime version. You knew I thought we'd be starting at seven, not three o'clock *in the morning.*'

He shrugged. 'I did think it would be a fun joke. But…'

His frown had things inside of her crashing and protesting.

'Frankie, if you have your heart set on picking grapes in the sun, we can do that too. It is just that the night picking feels somehow special and I thought you might like to be a part of that. I know there will be no sun, but there'll be a moon. And a sunrise that will make you glad to be alive.'

'I *am* glad to be a part of it.' She gestured

around. '*This* is what I meant when I said I wanted to have adventures this summer.' It'd be something she could to tell her friends and family about when she returned home. Learning new things and being part of something so totally foreign to her everyday world.

'We might not get sunlight,' she added, 'but we have moonlight.' She stared upwards. 'And stars. You have the most wonderful night skies here, Dante.'

'*Si.*'

But something in the way he said it made her think he'd not taken the trouble to notice them in recent times.

'Come.' He rose. 'The bus is ready.'

The bus drove them to a part of the vineyard she hadn't yet explored. Dante seemed at home here among the seasonal workers, and clearly knew some of them very well. Dressed in work clothes—cargo pants in a thick twill and a long-sleeved polo shirt—he looked like one of them too.

He looked at home in a designer suit as well, she reminded herself. But she liked him best in chef's whites, which contrasted with his olive skin and dark hair and brought the fire in his eyes to life.

Oh, stop it!

Clearly this early morning start was making her fanciful. What Dante wore was of absolutely no concern to her.

Arriving at their destination, she was given a pair of secateurs and a bucket, a brief demonstration of where she would find the grapes on the thick vines and how to snip the bunches of fruit, and then set to work along a row. While the moonlight was bright enough for them to cast shadows, floodlights had been set up at the end of the rows giving it all a festive atmosphere, like a carnival.

Dante worked the neighbouring row and something in her chest squeezed tight as she stared at him. He'd wanted to share this with her because it was special to him. In his own way, he was trying to thank her for taking on the role of maître d', and give her a little of what she'd wanted from her holiday in return. Most bosses wouldn't have bothered.

But then Dante wasn't most bosses.

It shouldn't turn her insides to mush.

No mush, she ordered silently.

He glanced up and caught her stare. She shook herself. 'Thank you, for all of this.' She gestured around. 'It's perfect.'

Those dark eyes danced. 'I will ask if you still feel the same way in an hour.'

Before long, his experience and fitness revealed itself and he had progressed much further down his row than she had hers. The night was cool, but when she finally made it down the end of her row, she had to swipe an arm across her perspiring brow. Her back had started to ache, protesting at all of the bending, and her arms felt like lead.

As if sensing her weariness, Dante appeared at her side with a water bottle. 'It is not as easy as one thinks at first, no?'

She drank long and deep. 'I think it's just as well you started me off on the night-time picking. It'd be so much hotter in the daytime. I'm sorry I'm not very fast. I'm probably the slowest worker you have.'

'Perhaps it is not so romantic as you thought it would be.'

She gulped. The moonlight and the stars, were ridiculously romantic and—

Stop!

He stiffened. 'What I meant is idealised. That perhaps you idealised it in your mind.'

'Absolutely.' She wished her pulse would stop doing that frenetic dance in her veins.

'Do you wish to stop?'

'Absolutely not! I've every intention of finishing my shift.' What did he think her? A giver-upper?

He blinked as if her answer surprised him.

He thinks you're an irresponsible flake.

She frowned. She'd channel less of the irresponsible, thank you very much. She'd given him no reason to consider her unreliable. A tad whimsical and happy-go-lucky, maybe, but not unreliable.

She straightened. 'However, if you've had

enough, then by all means feel free to leave. I don't need a babysitter.'

'I am not babysitting you!'

A pained gasp and low cry behind her had her swinging around to find Greta holding her hand and biting her lip. She was beside her in an instant and gently peeling her finger away to see the deep gash Greta had somehow cut in her left hand.

'My hand slipped and—'

Blood gushed and Greta swayed, deathly pale. 'Let's sit you down,' Frankie said.

Dante helped eased Greta down to the ground into a sitting position. 'I'm sorry,' Greta murmured in a mixture of Italian and broken English. 'It is the blood. I cannot stand it.'

Pressing tightly against the wound, Frankie murmured assurances to Greta while searching for the water bottle. She finally saw it on the ground not too far from where she and Dante had been standing and gestured for him to get it.

Instead, he reached down to Greta's other side and pulled out the one she'd obviously been using.

'Greta, look at me,' she said.

The other woman did. 'What I'm going to do is to pour water on the wound, and then smear it with some antiseptic cream, before binding it.'

Greta nodded.

'I'm afraid, though,' Frankie kept talking to distract her as she worked with swift fingers, 'that you're going to need stitches.'

* * *

Dante watched in amazement. Frankie worked with a deftness that made him blink as she cleaned and bound Greta's wound.

A small crowd had gathered and he ordered one of the nearest men to inform the driver of the bus that he'd be required to drive Greta back to the main complex, organised Greta's friend Stella to go with her, and arranged for a car to take them to the local hospital. He notified the hospital to expect them. He requested quietly that everyone else resume their work.

When Greta and Stella had left, and he and Frankie were alone, Frankie washed the blood from her hands with the water left in the bottle, and with a shrug in his general direction, moved as if to return to her duties.

'But you cannot just return to work.'

She turned back. 'Why not? Everyone else has.'

He moved across to her. 'You were amazing just then and…'

She raised an eyebrow.

He tried to find the words for what he felt, for what she'd done and how amazing he thought it. 'Are you not feeling shaky after that? You are allowed to take a moment to rest and regather.'

'The sight of blood has never bothered me.' She moved closer to peer into his face. The scent of amber and carnations rose up all around him. 'Do you feel shaky, Dante?'

'No. I do not like the sight of blood—it is the sight of catastrophe—but it does not make me want to faint or be sick.'

She eased away again. But he noted the pulse at her throat skipped and jumped. The incident hadn't left her unmoved, whatever she claimed.

'I just thought maybe you would like a rest and a drink, that is all.'

'I'm fine. Honestly.'

She set back to work and there was nothing for it but for him to return to the other side of the row and set back to work too. He kept pace with her, however, reluctant to get too far ahead and let her out of his sight.

She eventually gave an exasperated huff. 'What are you watching and waiting for? For me to keel over and fall into a shaky heap because I saw some blood. Honestly! I'm not that feeble. It was no big thing, okay? I'm sorry Greta hurt herself. But I only did what anyone else would've done.'

'No, you were amazing.'

'Nonsense.'

He halted and straightened. 'I do not understand you at all.'

She glanced up and then straightened too.

'You who are such a free spirit and so blasé and find it difficult to be serious for ten minutes at a time.'

She stared.

'I understand how you can be a magician in my

dining room, creating an atmosphere of warmth and welcome with your charm and your love of life. But that—' he gestured to where the incident with Greta had taken place '—feels at odds with who you are. How can someone like you be so efficient and brilliantly capable and…'

He wanted to tell her how splendid he thought her, but when he glanced back Frankie's expression had him taking a step away. 'What?' What had he said to put her in such a temper?

'In your world view, someone who happens to be happy-go-lucky and free-spirited is also unreliable, irresponsible, and incompetent?'

'No! This is not what I meant. I—'

'It's what you said!'

He stared. She was right. It *is* what he'd said.

A weight pressed down on his chest. All of this time he'd been badgering her to be what he wanted, while waiting for her to slip up. He'd pigeonholed her into this rigid idea of the kind of person he'd considered her to be, but it wasn't based on fact or truth.

His heart gave a sickening kick. He'd been waiting for her to let him down. In the same way his father had let him down.

Ignoring him, she resumed her work. Things inside of him ached and burned. He'd been spectacularly unfair. Frankie was not his father.

'Frankie—'

'I'm really tired of talking to you, Dante. I *don't*

want to talk to you. Can't you go and work somewhere else?'

This expedition, this night-time picking, it was supposed to be a special memory for her, and he'd ruined it with his small-mindedness, with imagining disasters where none dwelled.

'I will move to a different location, but first let me apologise.'

She kept working, not looking at him. He didn't blame her, but it made him want to yell—not at her but himself.

'I am sorry for what I just said, for all that I insinuated about your character.'

She still refused to look at him.

He swallowed, his gut churning. 'My father was a very charming man—*carefree* and *happy-go-lucky* were words often used to describe him.'

She stilled.

It took a superhuman effort to continue, but she deserved the truth. And he suspected the only way she'd forgive him was if he laid himself bare. And he wanted her to forgive him. Not for Lorenzo's, but for himself. He wanted her to like and respect him. He did not want to be the kind of person who let her down.

'My father was also rash, unpredictable, selfish and not to be relied upon. This is not you.'

Finally, she straightened and met his gaze.

'In my mind, though, I can see now how I have

conflated being charming and carefree with all of these ugly negative traits.'

She pursed her lips. 'It's why you don't have much of a sense of humour.'

He stiffened. He had a sense of humour! He—

'Or, at least, why you don't laugh very much.'

Is that how she saw him? As humourless? It was true, though. He rarely laughed. He rarely let his hair down and *relaxed.*

He shook the thought off to consider later. At the moment he needed all of his focus for her. 'I have refused to see that charming and carefree can also be paired with traits like reliability, efficiency and competence. I do not know why I have continued to harbour doubt in my heart when everything you've said and done has indicated that you are all of those good things.'

She stared up at the sky. 'Your father hurt your family very badly. His betrayal has been etched on your heart since you were seven. It's natural for you to distrust anything that reminds you of him.'

He hated that his father and the past could have such an impact on his present.

'Also, even I have to admit that not everything I've done since arriving here has been what one could exactly describe as responsible.'

He recalled the playful way she had slid his tie from his throat—the slow seductiveness of it—and heat coiled in his belly. 'I have wanted to blame you for the desire I feel for you,' he rasped out, keeping his voice low, 'but that's not fair either.'

For several long moments, neither of them spoke. Then...

'You now acknowledge that I'm reliable and competent?'

'And generous and kind-hearted.'

Some of the tightness left her face. 'Now *you're* trying to charm *me*.'

'Not really.' But the hard things inside him started to unclench. 'Will you accept my apology and forgive me?'

'I accept your apology, Dante.'

He believed her, but he could also see that her earlier ease and delight had dimmed, and that was his fault. He wanted to make her laugh again, wanted her shoulders to lose their tightness. He pretended to search for a bunch of grapes on the vine. 'I know how much you like making deals. Is there some deal I can make to help you forgive me more quickly?'

His words startled a laugh from her. 'Absolutely,' she returned quick as a flash. 'You can cook me breakfast.'

A smile built inside of him. 'This is a deal I am delighted to make.'

'Oh, and Dante? You don't really have to move somewhere else. You can keep working where you are.'

His smile widened. She really had forgiven him.

* * *

The grape-picking shift was only for four hours, and when the sun rose, everyone paused to watch it. The eastern horizon lightened slowly until pinks and pale blues began to colour the sky. The air warmed with the fragrant scent of wild grasses, but not even the tiniest of breezes stirred. All felt still and calm and expectant...and then the birds began to wake with chirps and chirrups and singing, and gold exploded as the orange orb of the sun finally emerged over the horizon.

Beside him Frankie gave a quiet gasp. He wasn't sure if he imagined her moving closer to him or not. 'Magic,' she whispered.

He couldn't help but agree.

Afterwards, everyone piled on the bus for the short journey back.

'Come,' he said as the exited the bus, turning towards the main building.

She trotted beside him, and he shortened his stride to match hers, reminding himself that one did not need to walk as if they needed to be at their destination ten minutes ago.

Frankie rubbed her hands together. 'What are you going to make for breakfast?'

He smiled down at her. 'It is a surprise. I hope you are hungry?'

'Are you kidding? After all of that grape picking, I'm starving.'

He couldn't explain why he wanted so badly

to cook for her, only that he did. When he'd been growing up, he'd revelled in feeding his mother and sisters, and his grandfather too when Lorenzo was at Riposo. It had given him satisfaction to prepare good food for them and to watch them eat it with enjoyment and pleasure.

He had experimented until he'd discovered his mother's and three sisters' favourite dishes. He cooked those dishes for them whenever they came to visit. And he wondered now what Frankie's favourite meal might be.

She halted when he left the path to head towards his car. He stopped two strides later, as soon as he'd realised he'd left her behind. 'Is something wrong?'

She pointed towards the restaurant. 'I thought...'

'The restaurant is closed today.'

'I know that, but... Then where are we going.'

He gestured at his car. 'To my villa.'

Her brows shot up. Small white teeth worried her bottom lip.

His gut clenched and he moved back to where she stood. 'Frankie, you have my word that you will be safe. This is not an attempt to get you alone or...' Was this inappropriate? 'All of the fresh ingredients that I had planned to use for breakfast are at my villa. Though if you prefer, I will return with them and cook for you here at the restaurant and—'

'No, no. That won't be necessary.' Her caramel-coloured hair floated around her face when she shook her head. 'I wasn't thinking, that's all.' One shoulder lifted. 'I'd like to see where you live.'

She would? Warmth spread through him. After handing her into the car, he drove back to the main road, turned right, and drove for three minutes before turning into his driveway. A well-maintained gravel drive took them up to the top of the hill, and then down a short slope to his villa.

Frankie leaned forward staring intently at everything. His stomach clenched. Did she like it? Leaping out of the car after he parked it, she skipped onto the lawn and clasped her hands beneath her chin.

Swallowing, he joined her. 'What do you think.'

'Oh, Dante, it's beautiful.'

He let out a breath he'd not been aware of holding. 'I am glad you approve.'

She glanced up as if suddenly worried that she might've said something that had vexed him. 'I thought—'

'What did you think?'

She coloured slightly and he leaned towards her, drew in that beautiful carnation scent deep into his lungs. 'Confess,' he ordered.

'Well, you're ridiculously wealthy, right?'

There was nothing ridiculous about money and security, but he knew what she meant. 'I have a great deal of money, this is true.'

'But this—' she gestured at his villa '—it's a

home, not a showcase. I was frightened that you would show me into some impressive mansion that was all glass and marble and I'd be afraid of touching anything because I might mess it up.'

He thought of the villa he owned in Rome where his mother and sisters lived, the apartment he had in Florence, and grimaced inwardly. They were definitely showcases. It was expected of a man in his position.

But, yes, Frankie was right. *This* was home.

'Do you have staff?'

'I have a cleaning service that comes in a couple of times a week.'

'But no housekeeper? No butler?'

'I do not want staff when I come here to stay. Here I cook for myself, and tidy for myself. Here I am free to simply be myself, rather than the successful business tycoon.'

'Then I'm honoured you've invited me to your home, Dante. If you're ever in Australia, I hope you'll visit me in mine.'

His chest expanded. 'I would be honoured to.'

CHAPTER SEVEN

THEIR GAZES CAUGHT and clung. The breath jammed in Frankie's chest and her blood raced in her veins. Today Dante had revealed more of himself to her, had made himself more vulnerable, and it had touched her in ways she hadn't expected.

'Come,' he said, breaking the eye contact that was in danger of becoming *too much*.

Hauling in a breath, she followed him. It didn't mean anything had changed between them. He was still her boss.

Except he was starting to feel more like a friend.

Inside the villa, she forced herself to focus on her surroundings instead of the jumble of thoughts in her head. The cool slate floors of the foyer continued into a formal living room, which flowed into an open-plan kitchen, dining and family room at the back of the house. It was all warm wood, pale green tones and simple furnishings, and she just wanted to sink into it all.

The floor-to-ceiling plate glass windows that made up the entire back wall, overlooked a view even more spectacular than the one at Lorenzo's.

Dante came to stand beside her and she gestured to the left. 'Are they Riposo vines?'

'*Si.* The villa is located on the western boundary of the vineyard.'

In front of them a gentle slope meandered down to a river that sparkled in the sunlight. 'I bet you swam there as a child.'

'I still swim there. Especially on the days when I help bring in the harvest.'

Her mind flashed to him in a pair of swimming trunks, and she swallowed.

'Do you swim, Frankie?'

'I love to swim.' Not that she'd done much of it over the last few years.

'If you like, after breakfast we could go for a swim. If it is something you would find agreeable.'

Clasping her hands at her waist, she forced her gaze to remain on the view, while the surface of her skin skittered with an electrical charge. To have a chance to see Dante in a swimsuit...

She moistened suddenly parched lips. It'd be undoubtedly dangerous, but they'd agreed nothing could *happen* between them. And there was no harm in just looking. 'I didn't bring a swimsuit.'

'My sisters have swimsuits here.' He turned away with a shrug. 'You could borrow one of theirs if you like. Why don't you look at the rest of the house while I get breakfast started?' He gestured back the way they'd come. 'If you turn

right at the hallway, you'll find the bedrooms—
there are five of them. To the left is my office and
the media room.'

When he turned back, those dark eyes took her
in in one comprehensive glance that left her burning. 'You are a similar size to Maria, I think. Hers
is the first room you will come to.'

Nodding, she shot down the hallway, needing
a moment to compose herself.

Get a grip.

His gaze had been dispassionate. He was cooking her breakfast. That was all.

She found both Maria's room and a swimsuit
without any trouble at all. She stared at the tiny
bikini and then shoved it back into its drawer.
Oh, Lord! She'd never worn anything like that in
her life. A staid and comfortable one-piece was
more her style.

And look where your usual style has got you.

Ha! That was true enough. A bikini could be…
an adventure.

Not that she really expected they'd go swimming. He was only being polite. A man like Dante
didn't take time off to go swimming during office hours.

The bedrooms were all of a generous size, and
the bathroom was enormous with its double van-
ities, which would've come in very handy with
three sisters in the house.

She moved to the door at the very end of the

corridor. Holding her breath, she pushed it open. This had to be Dante's room. It smelled like him—all citrus sunshine with a touch of sage— but it also hinted at the side of the man she'd witnessed on the hillside this morning. A man who clearly felt things deeply. A man who admitted when he was wrong and did what he could to make amends. Dante might work too hard, but beneath that serious exterior beat a kind heart.

She frowned, trying to work out how a room could say so much. Perhaps it was in its sheer simplicity. There was no ostentation here, no pretension. This was a room designed for comfort. And rest—*riposo*.

An enormous bed covered in a comforter patterned in golds and browns looked out onto the same view she'd just admired from the living room. She could imagine sitting in that bed, sipping coffee, reading the paper, enjoying that view.

To have weekends where you could enjoy such things. What a life that would be.

Tension coiled through her as she continued staring at Dante's bed. It was huge. The comforter and piles of pillows promised softness and warmth. She fought the temptation to lie in the middle of it all to see if it was everything it promised. If Dante came looking for her and found her lying on his bed… She gulped. That'd be ten times worse than pulling his tie free from his collar or impulsively hugging him.

She jumped when a text pinged on her phone. She opened it to find a picture of Audrey bent over an embroidery frame. Beneath her fingers the most beautiful design in silver and blue was emerging. The text read:

Aunt Beatrice snapped this when I wasn't looking.

Which made Frankie laugh. Audrey wouldn't notice an earthquake when she was immersed in a project like that.

Nonna has given me such a gift. It's a joy to be studying under an expert like Madame De Luca.

Frankie pressed a hand to her heart. Audrey deserved every good thing, and the chance to follow *her* passion for a change.

Thank you for doing this for her, Nonna.

With one last glance at the bed, Frankie backed out of the room and closed the door.

Heading back to the kitchen, her nose twitched in appreciation. 'Something smells amazing,' she said, sliding onto a stool at the kitchen island.

Dante shot her a smile, though his gaze remained on the simmering contents of the pan in front of him.

'What are you making?'

'Baked eggs and sausage. It is nice and hearty after all of the hard work you have put in for the day. Should help to keep you going for the rest of the day too.'

Her mind immediately supplied her with multiple visions of what she could do with all of that extra energy. Gulping, she wrenched her mind back. 'What can I do to help?'

He sent her a swift glance and she tensed. Could he sense the vicarious thrill that seeing his bedroom had given her? Did he sense the guilt and temptation warring inside her?

She sagged when he turned his attention to cracking eggs into the skillet. 'There is nothing to do.' After placing the skillet into the oven, he cut thick slices from a crusty loaf and placed them under the grill to toast.

She gestured at the bread. 'Let me guess, home-made?'

'But of course.' Tiny gold flecks rested deep inside the dark irises of his eyes and for some reason they made things inside her unclench. She shook herself. Carefree and happy-go-lucky. She'd live in the moment and enjoy herself.

They ate on the terrace in the warm summer air, with the scents of grass and wildflowers drifting around them and that splendid view spread in front of them. And the food... After her first bite, Frankie was transported. Dante had a rare and wonderful gift, and she didn't know what lucky star had shone down on her to bestow on her such an experience, but she silently thanked it.

Closing her eyes, she tried to savour it the way he'd taught her to savour wine. The sausage was smoke and spice perfection, the tomato sauce tangy and flavoured with garlic and basil and other things she couldn't identify and the eggs perfectly poached within it.

With a start, she recalled her manners. 'This is *so good*.'

'I am glad you think so.'

She reached for her toast, which in itself was every good thing, and swirled it through the sauce.

'I thought you might like to know that I rang the hospital and they told me Greta is fine. She needed four stitches.'

When had he done that? When she'd been snooping around his bedroom? 'I'm glad she's okay.'

Maybe they should've gone to the hospital with Greta? She'd have liked to have overseen Greta's care herself. She swallowed. Except, for the next three months, she didn't want to step a single foot inside a hospital. Still, it didn't stop her from feeling a little wistful.

His gaze sharpened. 'They told me that the wound had been remarkably clean and bound most professionally.'

Lifting her toast, she bit into it, pretended to concentrate on eating.

'Why?'

She did all she could to look baffled. 'Why what?'

He spread his hands. 'Why did you know what to do? You reacted so quickly. Why did you have both antiseptic cream and a bandage on your person?'

'Oh, that.' She waved the words off as if they were of no consequence, but her chest started to clench. He wasn't going to allow her to brush this off, was he? She didn't have to tell him the whole truth, though. Maybe it was silly, but she didn't want anyone here knowing what she really did, didn't want them calling her Dr Weaver.

When people discovered she was a doctor they immediately thought she had all the answers, believed she had her life together and mapped out and that the path at her feet was clear and straight. They believed she had her vocation and that she would sacrifice all to it.

All of that felt like a lie.

This summer she just wanted to be herself, not Dr Weaver, straight-A student, serious and hard-working junior doctor.

'Frankie?'

'Before I left home, I did a first aid course. Seemed wise,' she added in answer to his raised eyebrow. 'It was one of those accredited ones.'

She tried not to wince. She was downplaying her skills not aggrandising them. The fib wasn't meant to furnish her with some kind of advantage. It wasn't a lie for gain.

Her conscience raised an eyebrow. She did what she could to ignore it. 'And, of course, I did my research about the equipment I would need for grape picking.'

He blinked. 'You did?'

He really thought her both reckless and feckless, didn't he?

'Before I left home, I packed a tube of cream and a couple of bandages as a precaution. A stitch in time and all that. I didn't want some little mishap ruining my holiday.'

'I see.'

He looked totally perplexed. Before he could ask her any further questions, she rushed in. 'So, if someone sprains an ankle or gets a tick, I'm your go-to girl.'

She held her breath, crossing her fingers and hoping he'd accept what she said and let the matter drop.

'It appears both I and Riposo were most fortunate that you decided to spend a portion of your summer here,' he finally said.

The tension in her shoulders eased. She tried to not let them sag too much, though. She didn't want to make him suspicious.

'Coffee?'

'Yes please!'

She helped him clear the table, and then they sat

on the big comfy sofa as they waited for the coffee to brew. She rested her head back and stared at the view. 'You live in paradise, Dante.'

'*Si*. If only I could spend more of my time here.'

She meant to lift her head to look at him, there was something in his voice, but her head had grown too heavy. 'If you've given yourself the summer to establish Lorenzo's,' she stifled a yawn, 'then you need to make the most of it.'

And that was the last thing she remembered.

Two hours later she stirred and rolled to her side, blinked her eyes open to find herself staring into Dante's espresso dark ones. He had one of those L-shaped sofas and they'd both stretched out—her on the shorter side and him on the longer one—and had fallen asleep. Or, at least, she had.

That gaze didn't waver from hers, and then it lowered to her lips and his eyes grew darker, his nostrils flared and hunger raced across his face. Things low in her belly clenched and turned to warm honey. Those dark eyes moved back to hers and the air around them seemed to still as she hovered between breaths.

Dante wanted her. He wanted her with a fire and a hunger that made her pulse leap. And staring into those potent eyes, she knew he could see how much she wanted him. It would be so easy to reach across and—

'I'm sorry!' She shot into a sitting position—or tried to, getting tangled in the light throw he'd draped over her. Wrestling with it, she finally managed to wrest herself free. 'I didn't mean to fall asleep.' He'd said that there were *many* reasons he could not—why he would not—act upon the desire he felt for her.

She wanted adventure and fun this summer, but she didn't want to be anyone's regret.

'We were up at an early hour, Frankie. A nap did neither one of us any harm.'

But what about work? She might have Monday through Wednesday free, but he didn't.

Dark eyes smouldered. 'Would you like to go for that swim now?'

The smile he sent her was pure predatory challenge and, in the space of a heartbeat, she knew he'd changed his mind. He'd decided to give in to his desire. He now had every intention of pursuing her with every sensual weapon in his armoury.

Her heart started beating too hard and too fast. Was she going to allow him to catch her?

Very slowly, she smiled. 'A swim sounds perfect.'

Dante knew it was foolhardy. There were myriad reasons why he should resist what he felt for Frankie.

But something had changed between them on the hillside beneath the starlight. Something as fresh and promising as a new day. Resisting it felt more like an act of perversity than a sensible decision. He knew it made no sense. He made decisions with a cold and clear business head, but in this one instance, he decided to allow his instincts their head.

They rushed to don swimsuits, and he tried to hide his disappointment when Frankie appeared in his living room with her body covered in a full-length sarong. Still, it left those beautiful shoulders exposed and he could imagine running his hands along them, bending her back so he could press kisses against the soft flesh of her throat.

He went hard in an instant, recalling the way she'd pressed and arched against him that day in his office. His gaze fixed on her mouth. He wanted to know what she tasted like, he wanted—

'Swimming!' Frankie croaked and he slammed back to the present.

At this rate they wouldn't make it down to the river at all. Without another word, he ushered her through the glass sliding doors and gestured towards the path they should take.

'I wholly approve of this, Dante.'

He stumbled. She knew what he planned? What he wanted?

Dio! Of course she knew. She'd known the moment she'd opened her eyes and found him staring at her so hungrily.

'I think it's beyond time the boss started playing hooky.'

His brows beetled. 'Hooky?'

'It means to sneakily take a day off work.'

'And why do you approve of this.'

'Because you work too hard and your blood pressure is probably in danger of going through the roof. That's in my expert "I've done a first aid course" capacity, of course,' she added gaily.

'Of course.'

He smiled because he knew it was expected, but her words needled him. Had he misread her wholehearted approval of this swim, not as a prelude to something more sensually satisfying but as concern for his health?

His jaw clenched. He would do his utmost to correct this mistake as soon as they were in the water. He would leave her in no doubt of what he wanted. And if she wanted it too…? Things inside him throbbed and burned.

If she didn't.

He tried to quell the throbbing and burning. If she didn't, he would walk away.

When they reached the river, he dropped their towels beneath the spreading shade of a large hazel tree, pulled his T-shirt over his head and dove straight into the water. The sudden shock of cold had his body tingling, helping to temper his rising need.

He turned back to watch Frankie unwind the sarong from around her body to reveal the bright blue bikini underneath. Long legs, gently flared hips, achingly generous breasts had his breath jamming. But it was the sparkle in those blue eyes that undid him—that made him hope; that had him noticing colours more vividly and scents more keenly, and the touch of the water against his skin.

He ought to dunk his head to try and cool off again, but he couldn't look away as she hip-swayed down to the water's edge, paused as her feet touched the water. Bending at the waist, she wet her hands, giving him a perfect view of the breasts he hungered to mould and curve against him, before she straightened again. Sending him a big smile, she dove into the water just as he had.

A moment later she emerged just in front of him, water streaming from her face. She opened her eyes and her gaze speared straight into his. As if she'd sensed him there. 'This was a most excellent idea, Dante.'

'Why? Because I am playing hooky?'

Her eyes never left his. 'Because it means I can do this.'

She reached out and slid her hands along his shoulders, and the breath hissed from his lungs. She wanted him! He had not misread her intentions. He—

A shock of cold encompassed him when her hands suddenly went to his head and she shoved him under the water in a playful dunk.

Laughing, he bobbed back up and reached out for her but she was too quick and his fingertips merely grazed her shoulder. Leaving his fingers hungry for more.

In two quick strokes he reached her. Grabbing her around the waist he threw her into the air to splash into the deeper part of the river. Her laugh when she resurfaced sounded like summer and made things inside of him stretch and unfurl as if he were a grapevine and she were the sun.

They frolicked like children. He didn't know how they could have so much energy when they'd been up so early and had worked so hard, but the sight of her and the sound of her laughter filled him with a vigour he'd not experienced before.

'Pax!' she finally laughed, breathless with the exertion. 'Oh, that was the best fun. I can't remember the last time I went for a swim.'

For the first time it occurred to him that perhaps Frankie needed her holiday. That it wasn't just grief and an inability to settle down that was driving her, but something more.

He filed that away to consider another time, because all his mind could currently focus on was the way her body bumped gently against his. His hands had gone to her waist, and he tried to tell himself he was just steadying her, like a gentleman would. He could touch the sandy bottom of the river, while she could not.

In reality, though, it felt as if he would die if he could not touch her.

Her hands had gone to his shoulders and she

made no move to push him away. He let his hands slide around her, his fingers moving across the skin of her waist to the small of her back.

Her breath hitched and her gaze flew to his. The ebb and flow of the water had her legs grazing his and he felt as if every atom of his body was alive and on fire.

'Dante.' His name whispered from her and he watched the rise and fall of her throat as she swallowed. 'You've gone all smouldery on me.'

But she didn't look alarmed or cross or as if she were berating him.

'And you are looking at me with big limpid eyes.'

Still she didn't move out of his arms.

'As if you like the fact I'm on fire for you.'

Her eyes went wide. 'You are?'

Very gently, he pulled her hips against his so she could feel the bulge straining in his swimming trunks.

A tremor shook through her, and the pulse at the base of her throat fluttered like a wild thing. 'Oh!' She swallowed. 'You said…' She swallowed again. 'You said there were many reasons you shouldn't give in to this temptation.'

'And now I think there is only one reason to continue resisting.'

'What's that?'

'If you are unwilling.'

Her eyes never left his.

'If you are unwilling, then we stop this now.'

A gleam appeared in her eyes and her hands trailed across his chest, as she leaned forward to press a light kiss to his jaw. 'What would I need to do to convince you that I am *most* willing, I wonder?'

He closed his eyes and revelled in the feel of her in his arms, the scent and rightness of her. The gratitude that she wanted him too.

'Maybe if I do this…' Her hands went around his neck to toy with the hair at his nape and it was all he could do not to drag her closer. As if reading his mind, she pressed herself full-length against him, the sweet curves of her breasts plastered to his chest.

Small teeth grazed his neck with a lingering relish and a growl ripped from his throat. Capturing her chin in his hand, he lifted her mouth to meet his—lips meeting in an open-mouthed kiss of such delicious abandon that before he knew it, he'd pulled her to him as close as it was possible for two still partially clothed people to get.

And she wrapped herself around him. Her arms around his shoulders and neck. Her legs wrapped around his waist as she moved against him with an abandon that had stars bursting behind his eyelids.

Dio! If he did not slow things down, he would disgrace himself. Swinging her up in his arms, he strode out of the water and onto the bank. Capturing her gaze in his, he set her feet to the ground, clenching his hands at his sides. 'I have never wanted a woman with the passion I want you, Frankie.'

A breath shuddered out of her. 'The feeling is mutual, Dante. And this feeling of losing control…it's not what I'd call comfortable.'

'Oh, I can ensure that it will be *very* satisfying, though.' He'd make her come so hard his name would be drawn from the very depths of her being.

Neither one of them moved. She glanced to where their towels were, and then around the clearing. 'It's very private here.'

'*Si.*'

'I've never made love outside before.'

Mio Dio!

She pressed a finger to his chest, the light in her eyes flaring. 'Please tell me you had the forethought to bring condoms down here with you.'

Her forthrightness disarmed him. 'It would not insult you?'

She shook her head. 'I was under the impression, from the moment I woke, that we were playing a game of kiss chase. You wanted to chase me, and I wanted to be caught.'

This woman, she was extraordinary. 'I did bring condoms. Not because I was confident, I was far from sure of you, but because I feared with you my control would be very thin. I needed to make sure I could protect you—protect both of us.'

'So…' She stuck out one delectable hip and his

mouth went dry. 'We have this wonderfully peaceful spot where we won't be disturbed?'

He registered the question in her voice and without further hesitation, walked across to their towels and spread them in the low dip of land covered in grass and wild flowers beneath the hazel tree. The sun danced through the leaves of the tree, dappling everything golden and green.

Turning back, he raised an eyebrow.

She studied the bower he'd made for them. 'Even if somebody were to sail down the river, they'd not be able to see us.'

'No.'

'This—' she advanced upon him '—is totally private.'

His chest clenched at the expression in her eyes. Rather than drag her into his arms and ravish her, though, he waited for her to reach him.

'Are you comfortable with making love outside, Dante?'

He could see how much the idea intrigued her. He reached out to touch her cheek. 'It would be an honour for me to fulfil any fantasy of yours, Frankie. This—' he gestured around '—is one of my favourite places on earth and it would delight me to share it with you.'

He'd barely finished his words before she was in his arms again and kissing him fiercely, and he could not help but kiss her back with the same wildness. He'd been afraid that her need would not match his, afraid his hunger would overwhelm her. But her kisses were just as fervent as his, her hands on his body just as demanding and he'd never been more grateful for anything in his life.

She pulled away, her breathing ragged, to stare into his eyes. 'You are such a kind man.'

Kind? *Him?*

'You have no idea what a turn-on it is.'

He shook his head. 'You are...' He couldn't think of a word to amply sum up the way she startled and delighted him.

'A surprising woman, I know.'

'You are a delight.'

Her eyes grew suspiciously bright. 'I think that might be one of the nicest things anyone has ever said to me.'

He kissed her then, because he could not help it. But as he stripped that tiny bikini from her body, he told her how beautiful he found her, and how she was absolute perfection, and as he lay her down in their hidden bower, he trailed kisses down her body, making her writhe and moan as he catalogued all of the delights he found there.

'Enough with the talking, Dante,' she panted. 'I—'

He touched his mouth to the most private and sensitive part of her, and her cry of shocked pleasure filled the air. He stopped talking then and applied himself to giving her more of that same pleasure, slowly building the tension inside of her until she was incoherent and mindless with it, and only then did he send her rolling over the edge into that starburst of oblivion her body had been begging for.

He held her afterwards as she slowly drifted back, feeling like the luckiest man alive.

She had called him kind. He had been called many complimentary things before, but for some reason her simple compliment had pierced beneath his customary reserve to burrow into his chest and make a home there.

She thought him kind and it touched him in ways he couldn't begin to explain. But it made him feel taller, better and more worthy than anything in his life had ever done before.

And then she rolled over to meet his gaze and the sensual determination in those blue eyes had all coherent thought fleeing.

CHAPTER EIGHT

'THAT WAS AMAZING.'

As Frankie spoke, her hand trailed down Dante's stomach to his chest…and lower, her touch sparking across his skin like flame. When she palmed him through his swimming trunks, he couldn't stop from arching into her touch, couldn't prevent his quick intake of breath or the tremble that shook through him.

Heavy-lidded eyes gleamed, and a wicked smile curved her lips. 'You're wearing too many clothes.'

With that she shuffled down to slip her fingers into the waistband of his swim shorts and tug them down. He lifted his hips to help her, and her gaze darkened when she stared at him, standing proudly at attention as if he could not wait for her touch.

Because he *could not* wait for her touch. He gritted his teeth as she reached out and ran her fingers down the length of him. He bucked when her fingers wrapped around him and squeezed, and her eyes widened as if in surprise that she could have such an affect on him.

'You're beautiful,' she whispered, moving her hand experimentally up and down.

Sensation pounded through him threatening his control. Reaching behind for the canvas bag he'd filled with drinks, snacks...and condoms, he tugged it towards him just as her mouth closed over him in the most intimate of caresses.

He swore, he jerked, his hand clenched into the canvas of the bag as his gaze speared to her suspiciously innocent one. And then she ran her tongue down the length of him before taking him once more into her mouth and it was the most erotic thing he'd ever seen.

His body moved with a will of its own and it took a superhuman effort to rein in the wild abandon that wanted to overtake him.

'Frankie.' His breathing was ragged, his voice hoarse. 'My control is very thin.'

Her blue gaze burned into him. 'I can't believe I affect you in the same way that you affect me.'

'Believe it,' he growled, holding up the box of condoms.

He held it deliberately out of reach and as she reached for it, he took the opportunity to reach up and close his mouth over one rosy nipple and draw it deep in his mouth sucking and lathing and grazing it gently with his teeth. Her gasp of breath and soft, 'Oh!' had him smiling against her silken skin. His free hand drifted down to circle and tease and tempt the soft core of her. She was warm and soft and ready.

And then she pulled away, a condom in her hand. Trembling fingers sheathed him. As she lowered herself down onto him, his fingers dug into the hips of her flesh and hers did into his forearms and she stilled as if wanting to imprint this moment on her mind so as to remember it forever.

A sense of wonder filled her face and then she laughed, throwing her arms open wide, those dancing eyes meeting his. 'You said working holidays like mine should be filled with adventures, but never in my wildest dreams did I imagine an adventure like this. Dante, you make me feel like some kind of summer goddess!'

He didn't know how he could tell, but in that moment he realised the devil-may-care attitude she'd assumed this summer was all a pose—a disguise she'd donned to see how she liked it. Tenderness welled through him then, taking him off guard.

But then she moved with a deliberate sensuality, as if she were indeed a summer goddess, and the ability to think fled.

Frankie had never felt anything like this before. She'd intended to focus as fully on Dante as he'd focused on her. He'd sent her soaring into a dimension that she hadn't known existed. She wanted to give him that same kind of pleasure, the same kind of release. The same joy.

But as she moved against him, eyes locked to his, the pressure built inside her again—a sparkling shimmer moving towards her far more quickly than she meant it to. She wanted to resist it, but with a lazy smile Dante pressed a knowing thumb to where their bodies joined and, with a cry, she found herself falling.

As her climax broke over her, she was dimly aware of Dante's guttural cry and the pulsing of his body as the shock of his climax hit too and it spiralled her even higher, his name like a prayer on her lips.

She didn't know how long it took for her to come back to herself, but when she did, she found herself lying on top of him, spent.

She must be a dead weight. She made to roll away, but his arms tightened, and a beautiful flow of Italian rolled over her as he told her how desirable and beautiful and magnificent he thought her, those large hands moving over her with tenderness and warmth as if he wanted to imprint the feel of her on his memory.

They spent the rest of the day in decadent idleness. They swam again before returning to the house and showering. Together. Which, of course, led to other things, one of them being Frankie's discovery that Dante's bed was every bit as welcoming as it had promised.

He made love to her as if he couldn't get enough of her. It was addictive and powerful and she felt as if she was an actor in some movie who'd stumbled onto the wrong set.

Not that it felt wrong. It felt very, *very* right. It felt righter than anything else in her life had ever felt before. It was just that this was as far from her usual reality as she could get. Her grandmother had been right. Frankie had been in dire need of a holiday.

Dante cooked a delicious late lunch while she raided his enormous walk-in wardrobe and borrowed a T-shirt that covered her to midthigh. He'd told her she was free to borrow anything from his sisters' wardrobes, but she preferred to wear something that smelled like lemons and sunshine.

As soon as she spotted the somewhat battered chess board, she challenged him to a game. When she soundly defeated him, he demanded another game. Which he won. They'd agreed to the best of three games, but somehow became distracted again. Lying side by side in his splendid bed, and watching the shadows lengthen outside, she couldn't recall a more perfect day.

Shifting her head on the pillow, she met his gaze. 'Should I be making a move to return to Bertha and leave you to your private space and time?'

'I would like you to stay the night. But if you

wish to return to your campsite, I will return you whenever you wish it.'

It was an effort to hide the delight his words gave her. 'I'm not ready for the day to end yet either.' She studied him. 'And you look all the better for having had a day off, Dante. You looked relaxed, your colour is good, and you don't have all of that horrible tension in your neck and shoulders. You should take days off more often. You might work weekends, but that doesn't mean you can't take a couple of days off through the week for rest and relaxation.'

He shifted up on the bed. 'You look and sound like a doctor making an assessment and giving me a prescription.'

Her chest immediately clenched, but she kept her voice light. 'How depressing. I much prefer to look and sound like a summer goddess.'

He grinned and it eased all of the tightness inside of her. 'The summer goddess has worked her magic. I have so many feel-good hormones flooding my system it does not know what to do with them.'

'And this summer goddess is trying to tempt you to take tomorrow off as well. I haven't been to Lucca yet and it would be lovely to play tourist with you.'

He rolled her onto her back, his body pressing against hers, making her come alive again in a heartbeat. 'You, my goddess, are a temptress.'

* * *

When they woke the next morning, Frankie fully expected Dante to dress for work and head into his office, but over a leisurely breakfast he said, 'And what is your plan when we arrive at Lucca?'

Her pulsed leaped at that *we*, though she ordered herself to be cool and laid-back. 'My guidebook tells me Lucca is very beautiful. I'd like to walk around and see that beauty for myself—see the cathedral and the palace, and maybe walk the ancient walls. But my real aim is to find the house my great-grandparents once lived in.'

'And you have not changed your mind? You would still like to share this experience with me?'

The assumed nonchalance fell away. 'More than anything.'

Something in his gaze softened and he nodded. 'You were right in your advice to me, I think. I will be more use to Lorenzo's if I am well rested. It will help me make better decisions and it will help me be a better chef.' He glanced at the shirt she wore—his—and his lips lifted. 'I am guessing you would like to return to Bertha for a change of clothes first before we embark on our adventure to Lucca?'

She leaned across and kissed him. 'Thank you, Dante.'

The drive to Lucca was exquisitely beautiful with the rolling golden hills and avenues of magnificent cypresses that the area was known for. Dante parked the car outside the walls of the old city, and excitement shifted through her.

He turned to her. 'Why have you waited so long to come here?'

'I guess I've just been waiting for the right moment. Something in Nonna's letter...' She shrugged. 'It's just a feeling I have, but I think she wanted me to find out about my forbears.' Though she had no idea what Nonna wanted her to discover. 'I didn't want to rush it.'

He stared at her and waited, as if he knew there was more. 'And I guess I wanted to feel at home or at least acclimatised to Tuscany, before imagining another life—one in which my grandparents had never left Lucca, one in which Lucca was my home.'

'Do you wish they had never left?'

'Oh, no! I love Australia too. But I wonder if there is a part of me that will feel an affinity here.' Was that what Nonna wanted her to experience? 'As if I belong. It seems a comforting thought to have.'

'And what if you are disappointed?'

She reached out and touched his arm. 'It's going to be an amazing day either way. It couldn't be a disappointment.'

He pushed his shoulders back. 'I suggest then that we go and explore the old city first, starting with the walls, and then walk the streets your ancestors would have walked. After lunch we will find this address of your grandparents.'

'Perfect!'

The walls of Lucca dated back over two thousand years, and over the centuries had been added to and updated. As they were over four kilometres long, they hired bikes. She delighted in the tree-lined promenades and the grassy areas around the bastions where children played and people picnicked beneath plane and chestnut trees.

The lazy cycling, the warm sun and the light breeze on her face made her feel alive, and one glance at Dante told her he felt the same. It made her want to fling her arms out and sing.

There was so much to see. To one side stretched a lovely view of the countryside. To the other sprawled the preserved medieval city with its winding cobbled streets, narrow stone houses that had stood for centuries—the cream and grey stone glowing warm in the late summer sun.

A smile curved Dante lips at whatever he saw in her face. 'You love it.'

'There so much I want to see and do. More than I can fit into one day. I'm going to have to come back.' Probably several times. 'I want to explore the cathedral.' She pointed. 'And I want to climb Guinigi Tower.' She wanted to see for herself the holm oak trees that grew at the top. 'But today I think I just want to get lost in the streets of the old town.'

And that's exactly what they did. Hand in hand, they walked along winding promenades, stumbling across beautiful architecture like the Romanesque Basilica of San Frediano with its extraordinary mosaic, and the ducal palace. There were gorgeous boutiques that looked as if they'd always been there and markets selling the olive oil, cured meats and honey that Lucca was renowned for.

When they became ravenous and foot sore, Dante, with his uncanny nose for hunting out exquisite cuisine, found them an outdoor restaurant in a beautiful square with a tiny fountain where they ate the best pizza she'd ever had and sipped a deliciously fruity red wine.

Staring around, she stilled. *This.* She wanted a life that made room for *this.* A life where she was free to enjoy good food and wine; one that made time for friendship, and more, with a handsome man; a life that made time to explore the world and marvel at its splendours. A life where she could have an adventure every now and again. A life where one breathed in the summer air, enjoyed the warmth of the sun on one's face, and understood the importance of stillness and gratitude.

It was not the kind of life her father or grandfather lived, and theirs was the one she was in danger of binding herself too.

This was the life her grandmother had lived. It was the life Nonna wished for her.

When her father had died, it had knocked her off balance, had sent her reeling. It had all felt so *wrong*. It was Nonna's death, though, that had brought home to Frankie the meaning of family. It wasn't until Nonna was no longer there that what family meant—*really* meant—had become violently and blindingly clear to her.

Frankie wanted family, she wanted to create a family, she wanted to love, nurture and celebrate *her* family. She wanted to follow in her grandmother's footsteps, not her father's.

'Where did you just go in your mind?'

She turned to find Dante staring at her. 'I was thinking of my grandmother, and realised something. It's not a place that can make you feel happy or as if you belong.'

'No?'

'It is how you feel in your own mind about yourself and what you are doing with your life. It's in those things, I think, where our spirits truly reside.'

Dante blinked at the profundity of Frankie's words. If asked, he'd say that it was at Riposo where he felt most at home. But maybe it was that he simply felt most himself when he was at Riposo. He allowed himself to be free there.

He stared at her for a long moment, tempted to ask her what it was she really did because he no longer believed her to be a mindless wanderer, but he bit the question back. He would wait until she was ready to tell him herself, unprompted.

An hour later, they stood in front of a modest house to the northeast of the medieval walls. It was very similar to the other houses in the neighbourhood—built of grey stone with a red-tiled roof, and pink shutters at the windows. Frankie gazed at it with wide eyes, her hands clasped beneath her chin. He recalled how those hands had moved over his body—a curious but compelling combination of shyness and confidence, and wondered if he could hurry her back to his villa and—

No. He'd give Frankie all the time she needed here in Lucca. He'd not rush her in any way. He pushed his shoulders back. 'Would you like to look inside?'

She hesitated and then shook her head. 'My great-grandparents have been long gone. And I've no desire to invade somebody else's privacy. It's just been lovely to have seen it, and to walk the same streets that they'd have once walked, to see the house where my nonna grew up.'

'I have something I'd like to show you.'

Her eyes brightened. 'You do?'

'It's a surprise.'

Tucking her arm through his, she grinned up at him as he led them along the narrow street. 'I like surprises.' She nudged him. 'You, though, I think, don't.'

'Surprises in business, are generally not a good

thing.' He liked to have all his bases covered—to be fully informed and fully prepared for all eventualities.'

'I was a surprise,' she pointed out.

'I didn't say I thought surprises were bad.' He smiled down at her. 'You have been a delightful surprise.'

Her answering smile was the only reward he needed. Frankie had indeed been a surprise, and as a rule he didn't like being taken off guard. But she'd taken him off guard in the most delicious way. He did not regret a moment of it.

They walked in companionable silence for fifteen minutes, Frankie taking in the sights and sounds. She'd often point to something she found interesting or eye-catching—a hanging basket of flowers, a tiny deli tucked away, a bright red post box. Ordinary things. But seeing them through her eyes, made them extraordinary. He found himself drawn to the way she saw the world.

He halted outside of a large building. 'Here we are.'

'A hospital?' She frowned. 'Why would you bring me to a hospital?'

He'd expected curiosity, not consternation. His heart kicked against his ribs. How long had it been since her grandmother's passing? Had she spent a long time in hospital? He hadn't considered that. 'We're only going into the foyer. There's a plaque I think you should see.'

Entwining his fingers with hers, he led her inside, scanning the walls for the plaque he'd found on his earlier internet search. 'There!' He dragged her across to it. He read it out in Italian, and then translated it into English, even though he suspected she'd understood every word the first time. *"In loving memory of Gaetano and Adelina Mazzini for their service and largesse."'*

Her fingers tightened in his. 'Mazzini? That was Nonna's maiden name.'

'I did a little digging.'

'When?'

'While you were getting ready for today's excursion.' Did she mind that he'd researched her family? 'Gaetano and Adelina are your great-grandparents.'

She glanced at the plaque again and then back to him. 'Did you happen to find out what the service and largesse mentioned there was?'

'Gaetano and Adelina were both doctors.'

Her jaw dropped. 'No way.'

'Yes way,' he said with a smile.

She gave a little huff of laughter. 'Surely this is something I ought to have known.' She reached up to trace their names with a finger. 'What kind of doctors?'

'General physicians. They lobbied hard for improvements to the hospital and provided several generous donations to help fund the improvements. According to the history of the hospital, they were central in providing a teaching centre to help train young doctors.'

'But that's…'

'It's?'

'Extraordinary.'

And yet he couldn't tell if she was pleased or not. He shifted his weight to his heels. Should he have told her about Adelina and Gaetano before coming here? Maybe she was more like him than she thought, and did not like surprises either.

But surely this was a good surprise? 'Is this not something to be proud of?'

'Yes!' She straightened, and sent him a smile that didn't reach her eyes. 'It's something to be *very* proud of. To leave such a legacy is something that should inspire admiration and…'

'Then why are you not filled with admiration?'

She wrinkled her nose. 'I am, actually. I think both Gaetano and Adelina must have been amazing people. I just don't know why my grandmother never spoke of them to me. And now I can never ask her.'

Families could be complicated. He should have considered that.

'But,' she said slowly, 'in sending me here to Tuscany Nonna had to know I'd find out about Adelina and Gaetano.'

Perhaps Frankie's nonna hoped that discovering two such admirable people in her background, would give her granddaughter a sense of direction and purpose.

A warm hand on his arm, brought him back from his musings. Frankie smiled up at him. 'Thank you, Dante, for finding this out for me. It was very kind of you.'

He could see that she was touched at the trouble he'd taken. 'It was my pleasure.' It had been no trouble at all. He'd exert himself in any number of ways to give her pleasure.

He immediately thought of all the illicit ways he could give her pleasure and his pulse began to pound. As if she could read his mind, her blue eyes turned the colour of sapphires. 'You're looking all smouldery, Dante.'

'And your eyes are limpid,' he murmured, aching to kiss her but resisting because if he did kiss her, he was afraid he would not be able to keep it within the realms of propriety.

'I think it's time to go home.'

Without a word, he took her hand and led her back the way they'd come.

He played hooky on Wednesday too. Not that Frankie urged him to, but she did ask him how he felt for having taken two whole days off. He hadn't known how to answer, other than to tell her that he felt rested and refreshed.

It occurred to him that he felt more rested than he had in a several years.

She'd folded her arms, a challenge in her eyes. The sight had heated the blood in his veins. Or maybe that was simply the fact that she was naked in his bed at the time. He'd wanted to ravish her, again, but she'd held a finger up and shook her head. 'Hold that thought, though,' she said with a cheeky smile as she slipped out of bed and tossed one of his shirts on over her head. 'We need coffee.'

He made her the strong Italian coffee that they both favoured and when he brought it to the table, he found her with writing pad in her hand.

'If you thought I'd not noticed the way you checked out the food markets and that lovely deli we wandered into yesterday, then you're very much mistaken.'

What did that have to do with anything?

'Your mind is brimming with new menu ideas, isn't it?'

How could she tell?

'Describe them to me,' she ordered.

With a shrug, he did, and she wrote each of them down. She asked sensible questions that had him explaining each dish in greater detail. She idly pondered which wines she'd pair with each new dish he created; he weighed in with suggestions as well. And the longer they talked, the more and more animated he became.

He told her about a recipe he'd been wrestling with for years, but still didn't have quite right—

that he continued to search for an elusive ingredient that would help pull it all together and make it amazing. He was no closer to solving that puzzle when they were finished, but having a chance to talk about it reinvigorated his passion.

She was right. Taking a little time off from the daily grind could provide unforeseen benefits— benefits that Lorenzo's would reap.

They spent Wednesday playing with new menu ideas and considering all of his plans for Lorenzo's. It left him both relaxed *and* invigorated. It felt wonderful.

And he had Frankie to thank for it.

She met his gaze. 'How do you feel when you're cooking, Dante? Describe it to me.'

He recognised at once that it wasn't an idle question. He shifted, eased back, considered how to best explain it. 'It is as if all of my instincts and expertise come together in a kind of dance. They fall perfectly in tune with each other and, somehow, they make of me their vehicle. It is as if, when I am cooking, I can do no wrong.' He shrugged, half laughed. 'It will sound odd, but when I'm cooking, it feels as if I could right all the wrongs with the world.'

She leaned her chin on her hands. 'That's sounds amazing.'

He reached out and took her hand, squeezed it. 'You will find your passion too, Frankie. I'm sure of it.'

'What makes you so sure?'

'Because you are smart and generous. You will work it out. Take this time your grandmother has given you, savour it. And then you will see.'

Her answer was to kiss him. Which, of course, was the perfect answer.

On Thursday, Dante woke with a slow stretch and unfamiliar sense of wellbeing. Turning his head on the pillow, he found Frankie already awake, and propped up on one elbow surveying him.

Her eyes filled with warmth and she leaned over to give him a quick kiss. 'Good morning.'

He pulled her back down for a more thorough kiss before releasing her. 'Good morning.'

She gave an unsteady laugh. 'You kiss like an angel, Dante.'

Holding her lovely body fully against his, he grazed her ear lightly with his teeth. 'Shall I show you what else I can do like an angel?' he murmured, moulding her curves to his.

He felt her quick intake of breath and the way her body melted against him. Pressing a kiss to his collarbone, she drew back a fraction. 'Before…' She swallowed and he revelled in the effect he had on her. 'Before you start something neither one of us wants to stop, you might want to look at the time.'

He glanced at the clock on the bedside table

and immediately stiffened. '*Dio!* It is after nine!' He *never* slept in.

But then he recalled the exertions of the night before and that explained why he'd slept so deeply this morning.

'As much as I want to stay here,' she said, 'I know you wanted to get into the office at a reasonable hour today.'

'*Si.*' It didn't stop him from considering going in later, though. They could have a slow lazy start to the day and then—

They couldn't. He needed to check in with Michael and then triple-check with all of his new suppliers to make sure today's deliveries would arrive as planned, and that everything else was ready for tonight.

They were fully booked for the next four nights. There was much to be optimistic about where the restaurant was concerned and much to celebrate, but it was too soon to rest on their laurels.

As if sensing the conclusion he was coming to, Frankie pressed another kiss to his chest—her lips lingering and warming him to the soles of his feet. As she made to push out of his bed, he wrapped an arm around her waist and tugged her back, covering her body with his. Her gasp and the way she arched into him sent satisfaction coursing through him.

Lowering his lips to hers, he kissed her with a ruthlessness thoroughness that had her moving against him restlessly, those clever questing fingers pushing him to the edge, until their bodies surged together and their cries of pleasure rang around the room.

Eventually, he dropped her off in the staff car park on the way to his own dedicated parking spot. She hopped out with a smile. 'I'll see you soon.'

She planned to come into the office for a couple of hours to check her email and any messages the staff might have left for her. The knowledge he'd be working so close to her for the next few hours lifted something inside of him. Reaching for her hand, he pressed a kiss to her palm. 'I am missing you already.' And then he released her before he changed his mind and tugged her back inside the car to spend the day ravaging her.

He set the coffee to percolate before switching on his computer. And then he moved to the first item on the day's agenda—rang all of his suppliers to ensure that nothing untoward had happened with the day's orders. The fishmonger told him that he didn't think the day's catch of octopus would fill Dante with much enthusiasm, but that he had some most excellent crabs. Dante began rearranging the menu in his mind to suit as he agreed to the fishmonger's suggestions.

In the office next door, he could hear Frankie moving about. He would take her coffee soon. Ringing off from the last of his suppliers, he watched as his morning's emails loaded, and as he read them the smile slipped from his face, his every muscle clenching.

Dio! This was a disaster!

Before he could move, a white-faced Frankie appeared in the doorway. 'Oh, God, Dante you're not going to believe this, but ninety percent of the waitstaff are claiming they can't come in this evening.'

He shot to his feet.

'And it's the same for tomorrow night.'

His hands clenched so hard he started to shake. 'This is also the case with the kitchen staff.'

She moved into the room, her eyes narrowing. 'This can't be an accident.'

He stabbed a finger at her, fury exploding inside him. 'This is what happens when I take my eye off the ball for a moment and allow myself to be distracted! How could I have been so stupid?' He whirled away, registering in some small part of his brain that Frankie had gone white, but unable to quell the self-condemnation rolling through him. He'd known someone could be trying to undermine him and the restaurant and yet he'd still—

He'd let Lorenzo down!

How could he have been so careless, so negligent? His grandfather deserved better from him.

'I have been selfishly satisfying my own desires

without a thought for my responsibilities or what I owe to my family. I—'

'That's not true.' Warm fingers closed around his arm. 'You've been making room in your mind for your plans for Lorenzo's, letting them evolve, consolidating them. That's not selfish.'

'I knew someone might be making mischief for the restaurant. *That's* what I should've been focussing on.'

'You have been! You've been checking your emails and texts religiously in case of an emergency. Checking in daily with Michael.'

Maybe so, but all the while his mind had been elsewhere. It had been focussed squarely on Frankie. The restaurant had played second fiddle.

'Dante, it's not unreasonable for you to take time off.'

'Says a woman who has no responsibilities and nothing else to care about except to follow an agenda of pleasure and distraction.'

Her hand dropped and she took a step away. 'I would never do anything to harm Lorenzo's. You must know that.'

'Must I?' he shot back. 'You don't seem to care what you do with your own life, so why should I believe that you care about other people's lives?'

She stared at him with eyes full of betrayal and he had to wheel away. In a far-off corner of his mind, he knew he wasn't being fair, but had he learned nothing? How had he had allowed this careless, happy-go-lucky charmer, who didn't have a care in the world, to turn his head like this and distract him from what was really important? He who had witnessed the devastation his father had wrought.

Just as his mother had done, he'd allowed emotion to govern his actions when he should've been focusing on duty and maintaining a clear-eyed objectivity. His mother had lost everything. And now he was in danger of losing Lorenzo's.

The thought was like a cold knife between his ribs. He needed to excise all emotion from his heart and mind if he wanted to save Lorenzo's. His hands clenched. He *had* to save Lorenzo's.

Pulling himself up to his full height, he turned back to face her. 'If I had not wasted all of that time with you in bed this morning, I would have learned about this sooner.' His voice shook, but he kept a strong rein on the roar that had started up at the centre of him. 'I have lost valuable time because I was hell-bent on pleasure.' He thumped an open-palmed hand to his desk. 'Well, no more! This will not happen again.'

CHAPTER NINE

WASTED?

The air punched from Frankie's lungs, making it impossible to speak. Dante considered the time they'd spent together these last few days *a waste*? An unfamiliar and shocking sense of betrayal held her frozen.

Very slowly, she shook her head. No, he considered them something far worse. He considered them a deliberate undermining of his mission to make Lorenzo's a success.

And he thought her a woman of absolutely no substance. While she—

She swallowed. While she thought the last three days some of the most wonderful she'd ever spent.

As she watched him pace, she had one of those epiphanies she suspected her grandmother had hoped for her this summer—Dante's single-minded drive wasn't only harmful to him, but to those close to him. And Frankie *didn't* want to be like that.

She who'd always considered herself a failure if she wasn't top of her class, who'd refused to submit work that wasn't her best. She stared at Dante and realised that if she continued on the path she'd set for herself, she'd become exactly like the man in front of her—a tyrant to duty.

She knew something else too—a summer adventure shouldn't leave her so soul-crushingly shattered. It didn't matter how much Dante's body could make hers sing. She didn't want to be with a man—not even temporarily—who could turn into a humourless robot and make her feel like she was...*nothing*.

He was busy barking orders into his phone, having clearly dismissed her, so she turned and left.

She didn't return to her office but made her way down to the staff quarters. 'Greta, I'm glad you're here. I was hoping to have a word with you and Stella.'

An hour later she returned to her office, cornered Michael, and bullied Dante's mother's phone number out of him.

Twenty minutes later, she knocked on Dante's office door and strode in without an invitation. He opened his mouth, but she spoke before he said something that would tempt her to stalk off and leave him in the lurch. 'I have a list of staff I've arranged to work in the dining room tonight.'

He blinked and straightened.

She held up a sheet of paper. 'This is only a temporary measure. You'll need to hire new staff next week. I also have names of those with kitchen experience if you haven't found replacements there yet.'

He took the sheet of paper as if in a dream. 'How have you—'

'You had the resources at your fingertips this entire time. Seasonal staff often have other skills. All I did was go down to the staff quarters and ask who had waiting and kitchen experience and if they'd be prepared to work in the restaurant this weekend.'

He stared at the sheet of paper and then at her. 'This is a very good solution.'

She remained silent.

He moistened his lips. 'Frankie, what I said earlier...'

She didn't want to hear it. 'Your mother and sisters are also on their way to help in whatever capacity they can.'

'They're *what*?' he roared, jumping to his feet.

Wow. Okay. Not the reaction she was expecting. But the thought felt somehow academic. She felt as if she were in a bubble where his outrage couldn't reach her.

Planting his hands on his desk, he leaned across it, his face twisting. 'They are *not* to be bothered with any of this! What gave you the right to do such a thing? How did you even get the number?'

Her assumed calm shattered. Planting her hands on his desk, she leaned towards him too. 'Well, as

I'm nothing more than an irresponsible charmer, getting a phone number is a piece of cake for someone like me!'

He had the grace to look momentarily discomfited. 'Perhaps I was hasty when I said that, but—'

'Perhaps?' She raised a mocking eyebrow.

'But you had no right—' he thumped his desk '—to drag my mother and sisters into this.'

She eased back and folded her arms to try and hide the way her hands shook. 'Why not? Because they must always be protected and kept safe? Has it never occurred to you that they might chafe against the constriction of the ivory tower you've put them in?'

'They want for nothing!'

'Except an occupation to give some meaning to their lives.'

He blinked.

'Except the knowledge that if you should lose everything, they don't have the skills to make their own way.'

He went hard as granite. 'I will *not* lose everything. I am not my father.'

A harsh laugh scraped from her throat. 'No! Heaven forbid you should enjoy even a moment of carefree fun without beating yourself up about it.'

They stared at each other breathing hard.

'Has it not occurred to you that they loved Lorenzo every bit as much as you did, and would love be involved in a restaurant created to honour his memory?'

'My mother deserves a life free from stress, worry and work.'

She stabbed a finger at him. 'Your mother deserves a life where she gets to decide her own destiny!' So did she, she realised in that moment. *So did she.*

'You make me sound like a jailer or a tyrant!'

'If the cap fits...' She gave a careless shrug, one designed to irritate him, but his quick intake of breath gave her no satisfaction. She hitched up her chin. 'If you want Lorenzo's to be a success, you're going to have to surround yourself with people who you trust, because I've found out why so many of the staff have walked out.'

His head rocked back. 'What are you talking about?'

'They were offered bribes. Or threatened.'

The pulse at the base of his neck pounded. 'How do you know this?'

'Because I received one such phone call not an hour ago.'

'From whom?'

'The man didn't give a name, though he was certainly happy enough to pay me a pretty penny to jump into my camper van and drive off into the sunset.'

He turned grey. Though she wasn't stupid

enough to think he cared if that's what she did.
Except he'd then need to find another maître d'.

'When I refused, I was told to take care on dark
lonely roads.'

Dante was in front of her in two steps, his hands
curving around her shoulders, his body vibrating
with barely contained emotion. 'He threatened
you?' That strong jaw clenched though his hands
remained gentle. 'We must go to the police.'

'I believe the threat was empty.'

'We are not taking risks with your safety,
Frankie. You will move into my villa at once
and—'

'I'll be doing nothing of the sort!' She stepped
out of his grasp. 'By all means alert the police to
the threats. And if you're truly worried about your
staff's safety, then hire security guards to patrol
the grounds and keep an eye on things.'

He stared at her, his hands clasped, and for a
moment she had an image of him tossing her over
his shoulder and locking her up in a tower where
she'd be safe. To her eternal shame something in
her stomach softened at the thought.

She shook herself upright, steeled her spine.
'Has your research turned up anything?'

The pulse at his jaw pounded. 'It is not my
father who is trying to sabotage me or the restaurant. My sources tell me he is living in South
America with wife number five. The children of
her first marriage are apparently keeping him in

check by maintaining a very tight rein on the finances. He is basically living in a gilded cage. I do not believe he has had a second thought for the first family he left behind.'

She rubbed a hand across her chest. 'I'm sorry, Dante.' It had to be the bitterest kind of knowledge.

His only reply was a casual shrug that didn't fool her for a moment.

It wouldn't do either of them any good to wallow, though. She pushed her shoulders back. 'I don't believe this is a business grudge either. It feels too personal for that.'

Those dark eyes met hers again.

'Tell me, Dante, who would want to see you brought low?'

He braced his hands on his knees for several seconds, before straightening again. 'Lorenzo's other family—the children and grandchildren from his marriage.'

Exactly.

'Do you think any of them would physically harm your staff?'

He hesitated and then shook his head.

'Or you and your family?'

Dragging a hand through his hair, he strode across to stare out the window. 'They resent us, yes. They are perhaps jealous of us, but I do not believe that they are wicked at heart. It always grieved Lorenzo that they would not accept us, but he loved and respected them. I trust his judgment.'

'Seems to me the best way for you all to pay homage to Lorenzo is by burying the hatchet.'

He swung around, his eyes flashing. 'Oh, and you make that sound as easy as ABC.'

'Of course, it's not easy! Few things of worth are.'

She gestured to the chair on her side of his desk and he nodded. 'Yes, please sit.'

She collapsed into it, suddenly exhausted.

'Thank you for finding staff for this evening, Frankie. I have an agency working overtime to organise staff to cover our shortfall but—'

'Why didn't you hire staff from the village?'

His head rocked back at the accusation implicit in her voice. 'Because I wanted the best. I wanted staff who were experienced and had worked in the kind of restaurants with reputations that Lorenzo's would also acquire.'

'And look where that got you. If you'd hired staff from the village, they'd have been loyal to you.'

As far as she was concerned, he'd been focussing on all the wrong things. But she doubted he'd appreciate her pointing that out. And as she knew she'd stepped out of line in speaking to his mother, she kept her mouth shut.

He sat, rubbing a hand over his face. 'I believe I owe you an apology.'

Something too bitter to be a laugh rasped from her throat. 'You certainly do.'

Shadowed eyes met hers. 'I apologise for ranting and raving at you this morning. This situation I now find myself in is not one of your making. I should not have blamed you for it or taken it out on you. I am truly sorry. I hope you will forgive me.'

She wanted to cry then because she knew he meant what he said, but she also saw what he wasn't saying. 'I accept your apology, Dante.'

And she did forgive him because she knew what it was like to be single-minded to the point of obsession.

'Thank you.'

She swallowed and took a punt because…well, because it was what this summer was all about. 'It wasn't one of *your* making either, Dante.'

That autocratic chin lifted, and dark eyes hardened. 'I have been much at fault. I should have been paying more attention. If I had, I'd have had a Plan B in place for an eventuality such as today's. I cannot allow myself to become distracted again.'

She pressed her hands together, her eyes burning. 'By, for example, having a holiday fling with your maître d'?'

'Exactly.'

She couldn't explain the darkness that wanted to descend over her, only that it took an effort to appear unmoved. Her eyes ached, her temples

pounded, her body felt as if it belonged to someone else.

'You are a very special woman, Frankie, and I
have enjoyed our time together. But now it must
end. I need all of my concentration for Lorenzo's.
It must be my focus.'

She found herself nodding, but it wasn't in
agreement—just that he'd uttered the words she'd
expected. 'It's funny. The shoe is usually on the
other foot.'

He stared at her as if he had no idea what she
meant.

'Usually it's me who gives the "it was lovely
while it lasted" and "it's not you it's me" speech.'
Usually to fun-loving guys who wanted her to let
her hair down and have some fun. Not that she'd
dated much these last couple of years. She'd become as single-minded and blinkered as Dante.
No wonder her grandmother had become so worried about her. 'I'm not usually the recipient of
the speech.'

He frowned. 'I do not say it to make you feel
bad or—'

'I know. Which only makes it all the more mor-
tifying.' She rose. She didn't have the heart for any
more. 'Time to get back to work. There's a lot to
organise before tonight.'

She turned and left—her chest aching, her head
throbbing. She wouldn't think about any of that
either—the aching, the emptiness, the desire to

cry. For heaven's sake, it was just a holiday fling, nothing more. It was always going to end.

Shoulders back. Chin up. Deep breaths. *Carefree and happy-go-lucky.*

'Frankie, I can't thank you enough for contacting me.' Ginevra Alberici reached out to take Frankie's hands. 'It is a delight to be of service to Dante and be involved in his plans for Lorenzo's. Maria, Sofia and Giorgia are beside themselves with happiness.'

Frankie squeezed Dante's mother's hands. 'I'm so pleased it's all working out. But you must stop thanking me.' Ginevra had thanked her every day so far this week. And as it was Tuesday that was at least three more *thank-yous* than necessary. 'It's you, Dante and his sisters who are making this work. Not me.'

'But it was you who brought us together and it is something I will always be grateful for. I should have insisted on this earlier, but Dante was so proud to look after us all. It was as if it was something he needed to do, and God forgive me, but I let him.'

'Nobody needs to forgive anyone. What you need to do is turn your faces to the future and not the past.'

'You speak very wisely. Come and see how Maria is doing with the tastings.'

Maria, it appeared, had an aptitude for wine.

She'd not been there a full day before confiding that she'd been secretly studying to become a vintner. Dante had been speechless, before glancing at Frankie who'd been setting the tables in the restaurant at the time. She'd merely lifted a hopefully speaking eyebrow.

He was arranging for Maria to now be involved in every aspect of the winemaking process at Riposo.

Ginevra was going to take over as maître d' when Frankie's tenure ended, while Sofia was working towards a business degree. Maybe she'd one day work in Dante's business empire. Giorgia, the youngest, had no idea what she wanted to do, but her delight at being back at the vineyard was certainly genuine. They were all of them lovely, and had embraced Frankie as one of their own. She'd miss them when she left.

When she left… A familiar darkness began to descend and—

'Was there something you needed, Frankie?'

She started at Dante's voice. Forced a smile. 'Greta, Stella and I are going on a picnic and I was hoping to buy a bottle of prosecco.'

'You need *never* buy wine from Riposo, Frankie. You have earned as many bottles of wine as you can drink.'

He looked so happy to have his family around him. It made no sense that her heart should ache so. If she could just extinguish the burning that took hold of her whenever he was near...the burning to be in his arms and—

Stop it!

'That's very kind of you, Dante, but—'

'Frankie?'

The familiar voice, so out of place here, had her freezing. Surely not... Surely she was mistaken... She turned. *Oh, God.* 'Grandfather!'

Dante had only a glimpse of Frankie's horrified expression, but it had him vaulting over the bar and landing beside her. This man might be her grandfather, but she seemed far from happy to see him, and he had no intention of allowing anyone to hurt or bully her.

No, that's a right you reserve only for yourself.

The thought had acid churning in his stomach. Holding out his hand, hoping to buy Frankie time to gather her composure, he said, 'I'm Dante Alberici. My family and I own Vigna di Riposo.'

'Franklin Weaver,' the older man said, shaking it. 'I'm Frankie's grandfather.'

As if coming to her senses, Frankie stretched up to kiss the older man's cheek. 'It's lovely to see you, Grandfather, but why didn't you warn me you were coming?'

'Your mother has been worried, Frankie. We all have been and—'

A crash on the other side of the room had them all swinging towards it. A man who looked to be in his sixties had knocked his glass to the floor and stood there swaying, one hand scrunched in the front of his shirt, before falling to his knees.

Frankie leaped towards him, catching him as he fell and Dante moved with her to help ease him to the ground. She loosened the man's collar and felt for a pulse. He was the colour of loose cement and—

'No, no, no,' she murmured under her breath. Straddling him, she started chest compressions. 'Defibrillator?' she shot at Dante, not taking her eyes off the man.

Dante leaped up and seized the defibrillator from the wall and returned with it, calling to his mother to ring for an ambulance.

Frankie took the machine and, without even reading the instructions, positioned it with the ease of an expert.

Dear god, he hoped she knew what she was doing and—

A firm hand wrapped around his arm—Frankie's grandfather. 'Give her room. She knows what she's doing.'

Dante held back, but remained alert for any indication that she might need assistance. He couldn't help flinching when the man's still body jerked as she shocked him.

She did things, checked the man's vital signs. Dante made a silent vow then and there to do an accredited first aid course just as Frankie had done.

'His heart has started,' she finally said, but she didn't lower her guard or sag or any of the things Dante felt like doing. Instead, she rolled the man to his side and tilted his head back and kept her fingers on his pulse and looked as if she was counting.

None of them dared disturb her. She looked utterly and completely in control. If she'd told him to get her a sharp knife, that she needed to perform emergency surgery on the man, he'd have done her bidding without question.

It felt like an age before two paramedics raced into the room and took over. She spoke to them in a language he didn't fully understand. Oh, it was Italian but filled with unfamiliar medical jargon.

He knew in that moment. Knew that Frankie was far more qualified than she'd let on. And for the man's sake, he was glad.

But why had she not told him? He rubbed a hand over his face. Had he really accused her of being an irresponsible gadabout? And why should such an accusation so delight her?

When the ambulance drove away, Frankie swung to her grandfather with a glare. 'Thanks for the help.'

'You had it all under control. You didn't need me. Besides, your training in such things is more up-to-date than mine. Come, come, Frankie, stop being so childish. Surely this incident has proved to you where your future lies. Go pack your bags and let's take you home where you belong.'

Frankie folded her arms and straightened to her full height. Dante had started to recognise it as her fighting stance. He ought to. She'd used it often enough on him.

'I have earned a summer off, Grandfather.'

'Don't be ridiculous! Don't throw all of your hard work away on a whim. You have a bright future ahead of you and—'

'I will return home at summer's end as planned, not before. You've had a wasted trip, and I'm sorry for it. Goodbye, Grandfather.' She kissed his cheek before turning on her heel and striding towards the door.

'You owe it to your family,' Franklin called after her. 'You owe it to your *father*!'

Frankie halted, but then continued on without turning around. Things inside of Dante throbbed and ached. What did her father have to do with anything? What difficulties had she been dealing with all on her own? Why hadn't she confided in him?

His stomach gave a sickening roll. Because she knew how focussed he'd been on making Lorenzo's a success. Because he'd told her again and again how he had no room in his life for anything other than Lorenzo's.

She'd been a good friend—had helped him gain perspective more than once; helped him find so-

lutions to all the problems that had arisen. She'd
gone above and beyond in her role of maître d'.

What had he given her in return? A load of
grief and castigation that she hadn't deserved.
He'd been selfish, self-involved and inconsider-
ate. His grandfather would be ashamed of him.

He swallowed. He was ashamed of himself.

His mother's touch had him crashing back. 'You
should go after her and make sure she's okay.'

He glanced at Frankie's grandfather.

'I'll deal with him.'

He didn't need any further urging.

He found Frankie slumped on one of her camp
chairs, her head in her hands. All he wanted was
to wrap her in his arms and try to make the bad
stuff go away for her.

But this wasn't about what he wanted. It was
about what she wanted. He was through with
being selfish.

He took the seat beside her. 'Frankie?'

She immediately straightened, her lips twisting. 'Have you come to demand an explanation?'

He deserved her bitterness. Swallowing, he
shook his head. 'I came only to make sure you
were okay.'

She looked suddenly shamefaced.

'No!' The word shot from him. 'You have nothing to feel bad about. Also, my words weren't
meant to imply I'm not interested. I am, but I

have treated you badly enough. I've no intention of forcing a confidence you don't wish to give.'

Closing her eyes, a long breath eased out of her. She looked exhausted, and a bad taste stretched through his mouth. How could he have treated her so cavalierly. This woman, she was everything that was kind and generous and he'd stomped all over her.

Those eyes opened. 'I'm guessing you've worked out I'm a doctor.'

Why had she wanted to hide it? 'You might not believe this, but I realised some time ago that your devil-may-care attitude was a pose.'

'You did? When?'

His skin drew tight. 'The exact moment?'

Her brows lifted at whatever she saw in his face. 'Yes, please.'

'That afternoon down at the river.' He moistened his lips. 'You were so delighted to be making love in the sun and playing the sensual goddess. Which you did to perfection, I must admit.'

She pressed her hands to cheeks that had turned pink.

'I'm not sure how I knew. It was just…' He thought back. 'It was as if in that moment you had fallen in love with life again.'

She pulled her hands away. 'That's exactly how I felt.'

Why had he not trusted his instincts? Why hadn't he pursued that line of thought and dug deeper instead of allowing himself to become consumed with Lorenzo's again?

She searched his face, her brow pleating. 'Do you believe in soulmates, Dante?

'No.'

The word dropped from him. He had seen no evidence of such a thing. It was a myth designed to sell Valentine's Day cards and encourage couples to spend far too much on weddings. His mother and father certainly hadn't been soulmates. Nor, he suspected, had Lorenzo and his wife.

Something in Frankie's eyes dimmed and she turned to stare at the grapevines. He stared at her profile and his heart crashed about in his chest. Surely she wasn't saying she thought he and she were soulmates? That'd be *ridiculous*. And yet his mouth went dry at the thought and a giant ache opened inside of him.

He pushed all of it away and lifted his chin. 'What you did for that man… I am in awe.'

'When you've had as many years of medical training as I have…'

'Do not downplay it. You've had an impact on that man's life and his family's in a way they will be grateful for forever. You should be proud of what you have done.'

She frowned and blinked. 'I am.' Her frown deepened. 'I am glad I was able to help.' She shook herself upright. 'It's kind of you to check on me, Dante.' That gaze sharpened. 'How are you, though? It can often be a shock to be a by-stander and—'

'I am fine. You do not need to worry about any-one except yourself.'

'My grandfather…?'

'My mother is taking care of him. Which I sus-pect means she will see him off the premises.'

'He won't enjoy that.' She stared down at her hands for a long moment. 'Franklin is my pater-nal grandfather.'

That explained why the older man had invoked Frankie's father. His heart beat hard. He didn't know why, but he sensed the mention of her fa-ther mattered. That it mattered a lot.

'Franklin is a surgeon—very well respected.'

It explained the man's aura of authority.

'His father was a surgeon.' She expelled a long breath from her lungs. 'And so was mine.'

When the import of her words hit him, a vice tightened about his chest. 'It is expected you will follow in their footsteps?'

She nodded.

He studied her downcast expression and his heart burned. 'But that is not what you want?'

'I always thought it was.' She sent him a smile that made his chest ache. 'My father died when I was seventeen. A car accident. You can imag-ine… It was awful.'

He reached out and took her hand. 'I am sorry.'

She nodded, but her hand gripped his as if it

were a lifeline. 'I made a vow to follow in his footsteps. I wanted to do something that would've made him proud of me.' She swallowed. 'And I wanted to mitigate my mother's and grandfather's grief. I wanted to give them something to hold on to.'

'Oh, Frankie.' He fought the urge to pull her into his lap and hold her close. He was through with imposing what he wanted onto her, though. From now on, he would take his cues from her. 'You were trying to look after everyone.' It is what this woman did—she cared for people. 'But you were barely more than a child. And grieving yourself.'

She nodded, but it was absently as if her mind were elsewhere. 'Nonna asked me to take this summer off, before I made a final decision.'

'Final decision?'

'When I return to Australia, I have to choose my medical specialty.' She stared up at the sky, though he suspected she didn't see how blue it was or notice the white clouds drifting past. 'I have to decide if I'm going to become a surgeon. Or not.'

He saw then what a gift her grandmother had given her—three months of rest and relaxation to clear her head before having to make such a momentous commitment.

'When I arrived here, Dante, I didn't even know if I wanted to be a doctor anymore. My entire life from the time I was seventeen onward has been focussed on study, on learning all I needed to know, and being top of my class.' Her lips twisted. 'Because, of course, nothing but the best would do.'

She'd burned herself out. 'Have you come any closer to a decision?'

'Not yet,' she whispered.

His heart ached for her. 'Frankie, that vow you made, it is not one you should hold yourself to. It is not one anyone should hold you to. You were young. It was a promise made in grief. You deserve a life that brings you satisfaction and happiness, not to yoke yourself to one that doesn't.'

'I keep telling myself the same thing, but that doesn't stop it feeling dishonourable to break my word. And you want to know why?'

'Tell me.' If he could, he would fix it for her.

'Because in my heart, I know my father would want me to follow in his footsteps.'

Her words cracked his chest open. 'You are not dishonourable. You are the most honourable woman I have ever met!'

She rocked back in her seat.

He dragged in a breath, tried to temper his vehemence. 'Your father, was he a good father?'

It took a moment before she answered. 'He was a good provider—we never wanted for anything. But I sometimes wonder if I really knew him. He spent so much time at work, and rarely made it to any of my school events. Even our holidays were

interrupted because of some emergency or other.
And when someone's life is hanging in the balance, how can you begrudge it?'

Would it really have been so difficult, though,
for him to have shown her a little more love and
attention?

'I don't want my children ever feeling that way
about me. I don't want to be that kind of parent,
Dante. Do you?'

The question had his head jerking up. 'It is not
a question I have ever considered.'

CHAPTER TEN

FRANKIE STARED INTO the dark pools of Dante's eyes and her heart burned. Her hand still rested in his and she tugged it free. 'Why not?' Why hadn't he considered what kind of parent he'd like to be?

'It is not a life I have considered for myself.'

She spread her hands. 'And again… Why not?'

She could tell he didn't want to talk about it. And if she was kind and considerate and sensitive, she'd let the matter drop. But she and Dante were beyond such things. Whatever it was that lay between them, it was raw and emotional. And honest.

She hadn't always appreciated that honesty and she suspected he hadn't either, but it was like the wind and the weather and the turning of the earth—not something they had any control over.

'Well?' she prompted.

Those dark eyes flashed, and she suspected that if she hadn't just saved a man's life, he'd have walked away. That strong jaw firmed. 'I saw how badly my mother suffered when my father left. I will never allow a woman to reduce me to those same kinds of circumstances.'

She gaped. *Seriously?* 'For such a successful man, you can be incredibly stupid sometimes.'

His head snapped back as if she'd slapped him.

'First of all, no woman is ever going to leave you in abject poverty with four children to raise. Even if you gave all of your money away to this hypothetical Wicked Witch of the West, you'd still have the resources, experience, and connections to draw a good wage and support yourself and said children.'

'But—'

'You'd still have Riposo and your family.'

He shot to his feet. 'It is not my family's job to support me financially!'

'Oh, that right only belongs to you does it?' She stood too, clenching her hands as heat rose in her face. 'What kind of paternalistic patronising crap is that, Dante? *Seriously?* You want to keep them as pampered pets who look up to you adoringly, rather than women capable of determining their own destiny?'

'I— This is— You have no idea what you're talking about!'

'Then ask yourself why Maria and Sofia have been keeping their studies a secret from you.'

He starred at her with throbbing eyes. 'I am not this dragon you accuse me of being.'

Unbidden, tenderness threatened to drown her then. 'No one thinks you a dragon. But your mother and sisters are aware of this deep-seated need of yours to take care of them, and because

they don't want to make you feel lesser or somehow inferior to this idea you have, or want to have,
of yourself, they've kept their qualms to themselves. It has been their way of looking after you.'

He collapsed back in the chair as if her words
had robbed his legs of strength.

'They want to help you as much as you want to
help them.' She sat again too. 'But, Dante, they
want to empower themselves as well. So they
never find themselves in that situation again either. But even if they do, they know they can
count on you. That's what having a family is or
should be about. Your mother had no one except
your father and the four of you children. When he
left, she lost the one other person in this world she
was supposed to be able to rely on. And having
no formal qualifications made getting work that
paid a halfway decent wage very difficult for her.'

He rubbed a hand over his face. 'She should
never have had to deal with all of that on her own.'

'I agree. But it's not a situation you or your sisters or your mother herself will find yourselves in
ever again. So let it go. All of you are safe from
that fate now.'

Those dark eyes lifted. 'When Lorenzo came,
it was wonderful. But even after he had legally
ensured we would always have Riposo, it still felt
as if it could all be taken away. It was very important to me to become financially independent
very quickly. So that if it was, I could make sure

we were all safe.' He nodded slowly. 'But you are right. I have achieved that now.'

'Lorenzo knew the power and worth of family.' She gestured around, drinking in the view, knowing she wouldn't be here for much longer to appreciate it. A chasm yawned open in her chest. She swallowed and ploughed on. 'He made sure this was a *family* vineyard—*your* family's vineyard. Don't you think it would make him happy to know all of you were here working together to make the restaurant a success?'

He blinked. '*Si*, he would like that very much.'

'I know you think you and your sisters were a complication in his life—'

'We were.'

'But you clearly weren't an unwelcome one. Maybe to his other family,' she rushed on when he opened his mouth, 'but not to him.'

Eventually he nodded. 'He loved us.'

'So why would you continue to deny yourself the love and joy that having your own children would bring?'

'It is perhaps something I need to think upon.'

He said it gravely, and she couldn't tell if he meant the words or was just trying to humour her. 'One day you'll meet a woman who'll change your mind.' And she could no longer deny that it broke her heart that she wasn't that woman.

What a foolish thing it had been to do, to fall in love with Dante. But an inevitable one, she now saw. Despite his drive to succeed, his obsession with it, he had a generous heart and an honourable spirit. And something in him spoke to something in her. He'd given her the confidence to explore aspects of herself she'd never dared to before. He hadn't mocked her when she'd made mistakes or made her feel lesser about herself. She swallowed. He'd allowed her the freedom to simply be herself.

'*Dio*, enough about me! I came to talk about you, Frankie. And yet even now you continue to give—to get involved in other people's lives and do what you can to make them better.' He glared at her, but there was no real heat behind it. 'You would be wasted as a surgeon.'

It was her turn to gape. Her grandfather would have a dozen fits if he could hear Dante now. 'How so?' she choked out.

'You are so good with people. You should be doing a specialty where you are face-to-face with conscious people, not unconscious ones. Like a...' He tried to grasp the air. 'Like a psychiatrist.'

Did that mean he agreed with the advice she'd doled out so relentlessly to him over the course of the last few weeks? Maybe he'd stop working so hard. Maybe he'd let his family help him more. Maybe he'd follow his dream and remain the chef here at Lorenzo's. She crossed everything she had that it'd be the case. She wanted Dante to be happy, even if she had no part in the life he meant to live.

His face lit up. 'Or a doctor in the emergency

department of a hospital. You would put your patients at ease and they would have confidence in you. Or how about a paediatrician? Children would love you! You would be brilliant at all of those things.'

She laughed. Partly at his enthusiasm, but also at this new vision he provided her. He clearly thought her capable of anything. He made her feel she could be whatever she wanted to be.

He sobered again. 'You have the right to fulfil your own destiny, Frankie. You were only a child when you made that promise to your mother and grandfather.'

She'd give the same advice to someone in her shoes too. She knew she would. But it didn't stop it from feeling dishonourable to break that promise.

'You have given me all of this lecture about family and what it should mean and how it should work. Why do you not demand the same from your family—from your mother and grandfather? Why do you not tell them what will make you happy and demand their loyalty and support for what you wish to do and become?'

Everything inside of her snapped to attention. If she went to them with a plan for her future—one that would make her happy… They might be disappointed that she wasn't going to be a surgeon, but surely they'd support her decision? They weren't ogres. They *wanted* to see her happy. They just didn't want her to throw her future away.

'Frankie?'

She shook herself. 'That is some of the best advice I've ever received!'

His shoulders went back. 'I would like to help you in any way I can. If there's anything I can do to help, I beg you will ask it of me.'

She ached to ask him why—wanted to wrest a declaration of love from him. But she already knew that wasn't why he wanted to help. He was merely grateful to her for her help with Lorenzo's, and guilty about how abruptly he'd ended their affair.

'What are you going to do? Do you want to walk away from medicine?'

He'd said cooking made him feel alive, that when he cooked he felt as if he could right all the wrongs of the world. Practising medicine didn't make her feel like that, but her knowledge and skills worked in tandem in a way that made her feel...'

True.

As soon as the word whispered through her, she sagged as the weight she'd been carrying for the last nine years lifted. Practising medicine made her feel like she was being true to herself, being who she was meant to be.

Practising medicine and being a doctor, yes.

Practising surgery and being a surgeon, no.

She didn't want to be a surgeon and pretending otherwise, forcing her feet to follow that path, would be a perversion of her truth and a betrayal of who she was.

Nonna had sent her to Tuscany to find out about her family. What had she discovered? That medicine ran in both sides of her family—her father's *and* her mother's. It was no surprise to find she had an affinity for medicine. It was no surprise to find herself attracted to other branches of medicine either.

'Frankie?'

She started when Dante's voice broke into her ruminations. She glanced up. 'Binding Greta's wound, providing the occasional bit of advice to the other workers—both the grape pickers and the waitstaff when conversation has strayed to such topics—and getting that poor man's heart working again, has all felt so natural.' She shrugged. 'I like that I can do those things. I want to keep doing those things.'

As she spoke, she could see the future she wanted opening up before her. She stared at Dante with what she suspected was sparkling eyes and a goofy grin. He grinned back as if he couldn't help it. It made her breath catch.

'I know exactly what I want Dante! I want to be a GP. A general practitioner who has her own practise.' She leaped up, clapping her hands. 'I want to be a *family* doctor.'

With a whoop, he jumped up and swung her around. 'But this is perfect for you.' He set her back on her feet.

'I can be a family doctor *and* have a family of my own. I don't have to choose one or the other.'

She closed her eyes in momentary thanks. 'I can be both the mother I want to be *and* the doctor I want to be.'

She realised then that he still held her hands. Her breath hitched and her pulsed raced. She wanted him with a ferocity that frightened her. It would be so easy to stay here, to resume their fling because she could see that Dante still wanted her—it was in the way his eyes darkened and his jaw clenched. All she'd have to do was make the first move and—

No.

She wanted more. So much more. To settle for less would make the pain all the greater when she left.

She stepped away, reclaimed her hands, ignored the protest sounding through her. 'I still mean to take three whole months off as Nonna urged me to. I've earned it.'

His gaze sharpened as if he'd sensed the change in her.

She ordered herself to remain strong, forced a smile. 'You do realise my six weeks here is up at the end of next week?'

He stiffened. 'You still wish to leave?'

She did what she could to make her shrug casual. 'It was always the plan. I have the rest of Tuscany to explore.'

'But you could do that while based here. *Cavolo!* It is why you agreed to work so hard for me and Lorenzo's. So you didn't have to work for the rest of your holiday.'

It took an effort not to hug him, for in that moment he'd put her first before Lorenzo's and she loved him for it.

Stay strong.

'I think it will be better this way, Dante.'

'You will come back and see us before you leave Italy altogether?'

She shook her head. 'I'm not making any promises.'

Dante beat the schnitzels with a ferocity that had Carlo, his second-in-command, eyeing him warily.

Ignoring him, he crumbed the steaks and dropped them into the pan of oil. 'Keep an eye on those,' he ordered, stalking to the door and peering into the dining room. His mother ably manned the maître d' stand, welcoming the diners with a warmth he could not fault, but it was not the same as having Frankie there.

Frankie was still out there, of course, though tonight she was acting more as a waitress along with all three of his sisters. She was the presence that smoothed everything—the one all the others turned to for advice and guidance.

The bell to alert the waitstaff that a meal was ready pinged nearby and Frankie turned with a fluid step, only faltering momentarily when her gaze connected with his. Her eyebrows rose, but she righted her step and moved towards the kitchen. 'Is there an issue?' she asked him, reaching for the dishes waiting for her.

'Yes.' Taking her arm, he began towing her through the kitchen.

She tried to dig her heels in. 'Dante, we have a restaurant full of diners!'

'They'll have to wait.' His temples pounded. Not with pain, but with something he couldn't identify. 'I need to talk to you.' He needed to talk to her *now*.

'Inform Ginevra,' Frankie shot at Carlo. 'Hopefully this won't take long. And don't drop any balls,' she managed to toss over her shoulder before the door closed behind her.

'What on earth can be so important you'd abandon your post in the kitchen and drag me out of the dining room, Dante?' she demanded as he towed her into his office.

'This!'

Pulling her into his arms, he lowered his mouth to hers, claiming her lips in a kiss of heat and passion. The taste of her, the scent... He kept his mouth gentle, his hands cradling her face as he focussed on trying to tell her with his kiss all that she'd come to mean to him. She melted against him, her arms going around his neck, and she kissed him back with what felt like all of herself.

The things inside him that had felt wrong became right again.

Kissing this woman was as necessary to him as breathing air. Having her near was like his life-blood. He was not ready to part with her yet. He had to find a way to convince her to stay at Riposo for a little longer.

Eventually the kiss ended. She touched trembling fingers to her lips. 'Why did you do that?'

'I do not want you to leave.' He swallowed. 'Frankie, please do not leave.'

For a moment he could've sworn that something in her eyes lightened, but if it did, turbulence reclaimed it almost immediately. 'You want me to remain for what's left of my holiday?'

He nodded. 'You did not promise your grandmother that you would continually be on the move. You just said you would spend the summer in Tuscany. Why not spend it here where you have friends? I will not ask you to work in the restaurant again. You have amply fulfilled the promises you made me. But you can stay here—'

'And when my holiday is over?'

He blinked. He'd refused to think that far. But... He swallowed. This summer was one magical season out of time, nothing more. 'And then you will return to Australia and become a GP and I will return to Rome and once again take up the reins of my business.'

She turned to stare out the window. 'You don't see any future for us beyond this summer.'

It was a statement, not a question, but the import of what she suggested had his chest clenching. Maybe it could be possible. Maybe…

He shook himself. The notion was preposterous. As he'd already told her, he was not the kind of man interested in long-term commitment or having a family of his own.

Frankie gave a soft laugh. 'Well, the answer to that question is written all over your face.'

'I have already told you—'

'You don't need to explain, Dante.'

He did not like the expression on her face, although it held not an ounce of remonstrance. She moved towards him and things inside him electrified. He wanted that beautiful warm body pressed against his. He wanted to hear her soft cries in his ears. He wanted to hear his name on her lips as she shattered in pleasure.

She stared up into his face. 'Are you really going to return to Rome?'

'Of course.'

She flung her arm in the direction of the kitchen, her face darkening. 'Have you learned nothing this summer?' 'You come alive when you're in there, Dante! Creating delicious meals is what you were born to do. Being a chef is your vocation in the same way being a doctor is mine. Why would you exile yourself to the city and a job that means nothing to you when you could be doing this.'

'Means nothing to me? My business saved me!' His head rocked back when he realised what he was doing. He was in danger of allowing emotion to rule him. 'It is my business that makes the real money, not Lorenzo's.' He *would* be practical.

'Life is about more than making money.'

'It is clear then that you have never had to live without it.'

Her lips pursed. 'That doesn't change the truth of my words. You're ridiculously wealthy and yet—'

She broke off, hauling in a breath. 'When will you have made enough money, Dante, that you can finally allow yourself to be happy?'

He thrust out his jaw. 'I am happy.'

Those lips pressed together as if to stop more words from spilling out. Eventually she said, 'We've both been away from our posts for too long.'

He hauled in a breath. 'You will leave Riposo as planned?'

'Yes.'

'It is perhaps for the best then.' If he did not want emotion and desire in constant conflict with rationality and practicality, it would be best if they parted ways.

She turned and left.

He had to lean on his desk and wait for the breath to return to a body that felt suddenly and inordinately heavy.

* * *

They all of them gathered to farewell Frankie. Not just Dante and his family, but the seasonal workers and Lorenzo's staff. The crowd made him chafe. He wanted to sweep her up into his arms and kiss her one last time, but with everyone there, he couldn't.

Even if they hadn't been there, he couldn't. He scuffed the toe of his shoe against the ground. Frankie had armoured herself with a don't-touch-me air whenever he was near, and no man of honour could ignore such a warning.

It was his own fault. If he hadn't ended their summer fling with such vehemence—all but accusing her of undermining him and Lorenzo's—then she might not be leaving now. But that knowledge gave him no comfort.

Frankie moved around the group, hugging and farewelling everyone, promising to keep in touch. When she reached him, she hesitated for a second before reaching up and kissing his cheek. He held her for the briefest of moments, but then she was out of his arms again. It passed too quickly. He had not even had a chance to imprint the kiss on his memory!

'Dante, it's been an adventure.' Her eyes danced for a moment before sobering. 'You've given me so much. And I'm not talking about the opportunity to make enough money for the summer,' she added with a roll of her eyes. 'I'm very grateful. I'll never forget you.'

Before he could make any kind of answer, she'd leaped into Bertha and started the engine. He swore she swiped a hand across her eyes. It took all of his strength not to pull her back out again and demand she stay.

Her lips curved into a smile, but her eyes remained suspiciously bright. 'I left a present for you on your desk.'

A present? For him? But why?

And why on earth hadn't he given her something to remember him by? He wanted to turn back time and—

But then she was gone and his entire body turned to stone and he didn't have the strength to even lift his hand in farewell.

His mother's hand on his arm drew him back. 'Dante—'

'Not now, Mamma.'

Turning on his heel, he strode off towards his office. He would bury himself in work.

It was work that was important. Not holiday flings.

Work would drive all of this nonsense from his mind.

Several hours later he glanced up at a tap on his door. Ginevra stood there with a plate of cured meats, cheese and olives in one hand and a basket of bread in the other. 'It's well after lunchtime, Dante. You need to stop and eat.'

He wasn't hungry, but something in his mother's voice told him she wouldn't accept such an excuse. He waved her in, made room for the food.

She didn't leave, but took the seat opposite, helping herself to a piece of cheese. He ground down a sigh. He should have known she'd stay to make sure he would eat. Seizing two slices of sourdough, he made a sandwich of cheese and salami and took a bite, barely noticing the taste or textures like he normally would.

Normal was nowhere to be found today. He had multiple files open on both his desk and his computer, but none of them had managed to hold his attention. Sweeping the physical files into a pile, he tossed them onto the bench behind him. Taking another bite, he set his computer to sleep mode.

Ginevra gestured to the brightly wrapped present on top of his filing cabinet. 'You haven't opened Frankie's gift yet.'

He did his best not to scowl. 'I'm saving it as a reward for when I have finished my work.'

'There's more to life than work, Dante.'

Her words were reminiscent of the ones Frankie had spoken. 'Work is important.'

'Not more important than family or love, though.'

'I agree. It is why I have taken this time off to create a restaurant to celebrate Nonno.'

She was silent for so long he shifted on his seat. 'You wish to say something?'

Shadowed eyes met his. 'I know what happened between your father and me marked you dread-fully.'

'*Mamma*—'

'No, let me finish, Dante. Just because things didn't work out between your father and me, does not mean that love isn't worth fighting for.'

'He broke your heart. He abandoned you and—'

'And I have found love again.'

Her words punched the breath from his body.

'His name is Roberto and you will meet him next week when he arrives for a visit.' His heart kicked at her sudden smile. It transformed her face in a way he'd never seen before. 'He makes me happy, Dante.'

'I am very happy for you, Mamma.' He came around from behind the desk to embrace her. 'I look forward to meeting him.'

His mother drew back, gripping his hands. 'Why did you let your Frankie go when you love her so?'

Love her? He didn't—

It was suddenly hard to get air into his lungs. He loved Frankie? But—

He loved Frankie!

It explained this darkness in his soul, explained why nothing made sense now that she was gone. Whirling away, he paced, hands clenching and unclenching. 'How did you find the courage to love again when it ended so badly the first time?' he demanded of his mother.

'Love, when you find it, makes your whole life better, Dante. In every respect. I fought it for a long time. But some people are worth risking your heart for.'

Some people are worth risking your heart for.

He lowered himself to his chair, his mother's words going around and around in his mind.

'Dante.'

He glanced up.

'Do you really think Frankie would treat your heart with cruelty and trample all over it? Do you think she is selfish and without compassion?'

He shot to his feet. 'She is everything that is kind and generous!'

And he'd driven her away.

Ginevra said nothing more. Simply glanced at the gift Frankie had left, before pulling a folded sheet of paper from her pocket and placing it on the table beside the plate of food. Then she left.

He stared at the note. He stared at Frankie's gift. With a smothered oath, he seized the gift and unwrapped it, his heart clenching when he unwrapped the object from its protective blanket. She'd given him Leilani. Her beautiful Hawaiian ukulele. The ukulele she'd said she'd aspired to play well. The ukulele of her dreams.

His throat thickened.

She'd left no card, but she had printed out the music and the finger chart for 'You Are My Sunshine'. Scrawled across the bottom of it in her messy handwriting, she'd written:

To play whenever you need to relax or are feeling blue.

He immediately began strumming the chords she'd taught him. And while his heart remained just as heavy, playing and singing helped to push back some of the darkness that engulfed him.

He played it twice before reaching for his mother's note and unfolding it. Everything inside of him stiffened when he realised what she'd given him—Frankie's projected itinerary for the next month.

Some people are worth risking your heart for.

He played the song one more time, staring at Frankie's itinerary. By the time he reached the end he knew exactly what he had to do.

CHAPTER ELEVEN

CAREFREE AND HAPPY-GO-LUCKY.

Frankie wanted to throw her head back and laugh—harsh ugly laughter. It didn't matter how many times she repeated the words, she couldn't make herself feel anything but heavy, sad...heartbroken.

'This wasn't part of the plan, Nonna,' she whispered.

Not that she'd stuck to the plan. When she'd left Riposo and Dante seven days ago, she'd been planning to spend the night in Lucca—to further explore the town of her forbears. But when she'd arrived, all she'd been able to think about was the day she'd spent there with Dante.

She hadn't even switched off Bertha's engine. Instead, she'd slammed her foot to the accelerator and raced out of town. She'd driven to Pisa, but that hadn't felt far enough away from the memories that plagued her, so she'd continued on until her eyes were too gritty to keep driving any longer. She'd stayed overnight in a tiny hotel in a town whose name she couldn't pronounce.

And now, today, she'd driven through ridiculously scenic Val d'Orcia with its rolling golden hills and cypress trees, and so much beauty it should fill her soul. The photo opportunities had been plentiful, and she'd dutifully stopped to take said photographs because it was expected. She'd sent various photos to her mother and Audrey. She didn't want anyone worrying about her. She wanted them all thinking she was having the time of her life.

She hadn't stayed in one place for longer than a night, though. Some nights she'd stayed in camping grounds sleeping in Bertha. Others she'd spent in a hotel. For the last two nights, though, she'd stayed in a tiny room at a Renaissance inn with breathtaking views.

Her phone rang as she walked into her room now. Glancing at the caller ID, she dragged in a breath, and donned a happy voice. 'Audrey! How are things? Did you get the picture I sent earlier?'

'I did. Thank you. Oh, Frankie, you're travelling through the most beautiful countryside!'

She stiffened. 'What's wrong?'

'Nothing! I just...'

'Audrey...' She used her bossy doctor voice. She knew Audrey too well. Something was up.

'Oh, heavens, Frankie, I hardly know where to start! You know the package Nonna wanted me to deliver to Aunt Beatrice?'

Aunt Beatrice had been Nonna's best friend.

She'd visited them in Australia several times. Nonna had tasked Audrey with hand delivering a *'very special package'* to Beatrice. They'd thought it was simply an excuse to ensure Audrey had a holiday.

'Well apparently that package included all the details of my mother's family.'

Frankie straightened. 'No way!'

'And, Frankie, you won't believe it but they're an old aristocratic family that goes back centuries.'

Her heart beat hard. This was such momentous news. 'Are you okay?'

'I...think so.'

She let out a breath. Audrey sounded shell-shocked, but not upset. 'What are they like?'

'They're so different to our family, Frankie.'

'Do you want me to come to Lake Como?' If Audrey needed her support, she'd be there in a heartbeat.

'Thanks, Frankie, but I think this is something I have to do myself.'

She understood that. 'Okay, but don't forget I'm only a phone call away.'

'I know.'

'If you need the cavalry to ride in, Bertha and I can be in Lake Como in under five hours.'

'That won't be necessary.'

Audrey's laugh helped allay some of Frankie's worry.

'They're going to love you, Audrey. I promise you.'

'Thanks, Frankie,' she whispered. 'Love you.'

'Love you too.'

Frankie stared at her phone when they rang off,
hoping with all her heart that things worked out
for Audrey. Her cousin deserved everything good
that life had to offer—including a family who appreciated her.

She glanced around her room, sat on the bed,
but the walls felt as if they were pressing in on
her. Muttering a curse, she grabbed Saffy and
headed back outside.

Carefree and happy-go-lucky.

Not knowing what to do, she wound down
whimsical cobbled alleyways until she eventually found herself in a square with a glorious view
of the early evening sunset. Planting herself at a
wrought iron table beneath a lime tree, she ordered a glass of white wine and forced herself to
do a meditation exercise.

It had been seven days. It was time to stop
indulging in self-pity and wallowing in such
sadness. She might miss Dante with the same
fierceness she'd miss a limb, but that didn't change
the fact that he didn't love her.

Nor was she silly enough to believe that she
could recover from a broken heart in seven days.
It would take a long time for her heart to stop pin-
ing for him. But that didn't mean she couldn't turn

her face to the future. It didn't mean she couldn't still enjoy things.

She was going to be a GP—a family doctor—and the realisation that it was the perfect path for her made her thankful. She focussed on that feeling for a little while—the freedom, the cessation of the constant, chafing stress. When her wine came, she silently toasted the sunset and Nonna. She'd accomplished what she'd set out to do on this trip—to decide her future. And that future looked and felt bright and right.

But Dante...

She resolutely pushed all thoughts of him from her head, picked up Saffy and idly started strumming. It was time to make way for fun and frivolity and simple pleasures again. They might not mend a broken heart, but they'd help it become easier to bear.

She sang 'Over the Rainbow', because, of course, it was *the* iconic ukulele song. She stared at the view and sipped her wine and tried to not compare it to Riposo's Pinot Grigio. Unable to stop herself, even though the song held too many memories of Dante, she played 'You Are My Sunshine'.

Eventually she became aware of someone to her left singing too in a lovely deep baritone.

When the song ended, a shadow fell over the table and a deep, rich voice asked, 'May I take a seat?'

Her breath caught in her throat. All she could do was stare. *Dante!*

What on earth was he doing here? Was it a co-incidence or had he come looking for her? If he'd come looking for her then why—

Of course it's a coincidence.

He sat and nodded towards her glass. 'How is the wine?'

'Nothing to write home about.' She couldn't believe her voice actually worked.

'That is an expression I do not know, but I can guess it's meaning.'

He took her glass and sniffed the contents before setting it back down with a shake of his head. Calling the waiter over, he ordered two glasses of a wine she'd never heard of before.

'Try this,' he ordered when it arrived.

She did and it was perfection. It tasted like moonlight and the stars and happy thoughts. 'Delicious,' she agreed, fighting the urge to cry.

'Have you tried the Pecorino yet? It is what this town is known for.'

He was here to buy Pecorino? She should've known. Pushing her shoulders back, she kept her chin high. 'I hope everyone at Riposo is well?'

'*Si.* Very well.'

'And you're here to buy Pecorino?'

'I'm here to find you.'

She blinked.

'You have been very hard to find.' His brow furrowed and he pulled a piece of paper from his pocket and set it on the table, stabbed a finger at it. 'You were supposed to follow this!'

She glanced at it. Her itinerary!

She glanced back at him. He looked enraged and baffled. She noted the tired lines fanning from his eyes and the deep grooves bracketing his mouth. Before she could stop herself, she covered his hand with hers. 'Are you all right, Dante?'

'No, I am not all right,' he shot back, glaring at her. 'I have been half out of my mind with worry for you. I have been searching for you all this time.'

All this time? 'Who has been cooking at Lorenzo's?'

'Carlo. He is very good.'

Dante had left his second-in-command *in charge* of Lorenzo's kitchen?

'Finding you was more important.'

The set of his mouth had her blood pounding. 'Why did you need to find me?'

She went to move her hand, but he caught it in both of his. 'Because you are my sunshine, Frankie. I was afraid I would never be able to find you so I could tell you that.'

He…

Was…

What?

'I love you, *cara*, heart and soul. It is just that I did not realise until you were gone. And I know you have no reason to trust me, but the words I speak are true. My mother called me an idiot for letting you go.'

Ginevra had…?

'She made me see that there are some people worth risking your heart for. And I do not have any expectations that you feel the same way about me, Frankie. But I think, if given a chance, I could eventually win you over.'

He had her heart, but her throat had closed over and she couldn't push a single sound out.

'All my life I have considered *happy-go-lucky* and *charming* synonyms for irresponsibility and recklessness, but you proved to me otherwise. In this same way, I have always considered emotion a bad thing—something that is misleading and not to be trusted. Hence the reason I have always focussed on work and practical things. But again, I have been wrong. The right kind of emotion is—' His face lit up. 'It is nourishment for the soul in the way a delicious meal is nourishment for the body.'

Her mouth fell open.

His hands tightened about hers. 'I have considered very closely the kind of life that will make you happy. I have researched how you can practise medicine in Italy. It is not straightforward… there are exams—'

There were always exams.

'Or you can complete your specialisation in Australia and then register to have your qualification recognised. This of course means conducting a long-distance love affair for a year, but I will do anything to make you happy.'

The lump in her throat grew.

'Once those things are done, however, it would be possible to establish a practise wherever you would like in Italy. And I will be your sponsor in every way I can to help ensure all goes smoothly.'

'I...'

'That leads us to where we would live. And I think that, if you are agreeable, we would live at Riposo.'

She tried not to gape. 'What about Rome?'

'Rome would not make you happy.' His eyes gentled. 'And you were right. I am not living the life that would make me happy. Not deep down in my heart. I will work on handing over the reins of my business concerns to my executive team. And then I mean to take over as head chef at Lorenzo's for good.'

Dante was choosing happiness over duty and security? The thought stole her breath.

'I have also considered the possibility that you would like to reside in Australia.' He gave a careless shrug. 'In which case I will relocate to Melbourne or wherever it is you decide to live.'

'You can't— Your family!'

'I love them, *cara*, but it is you who are my sunshine. Without you, there is no joy in anything I do and no meaning in my life.'

She pressed her free hand over her madly beating heart to stop it from pounding out of her chest.

Those dark eyes speared hers, holding her captive. 'You know what my greatest fear is, Frankie.'

She swallowed. 'To lose all your money and be left destitute once again.'

Those eyes smiled at her. 'The thought of losing you is ten times worse. If it would help to win your heart. I will freely give you my entire fortune.'

She shot back in her chair. 'You can't do that!'

One careless shoulder lifted. 'I know you would not wield it against me with cruelty or fritter it away in gambling or some other vice. You are an honourable woman. And if it would give you a sense of security to be the one controlling the purse strings then I would hand them to you without a moment's hesitation. I want you to know that I not only respect you, but that I trust you.'

The words he was saying, they were too much. Her mind blanked, but her body burned and fluttered.

'And maybe one day, if you decide you love me too, we could have children.'

Her eyes filled.

He gripped both her hands, suddenly urgent. 'Please, Frankie, tell me that I at least have a chance of winning your heart? I will do—'

Reaching across she pressed her fingers to his lips. 'Dante, you cannot win what is already yours. I love you with every part of myself, and I want the life you describe to me with all of my being.'

He stared at her in incomprehension, clearly not expecting such an answer, and then his face lit up with such delight it heated her blood. And then she was in his arms and he was kissing her with such fervent gratitude her head spun. She didn't know how long it was before he lifted his head, but her entire body fizzed with desire and happiness.

'You will come home with me tonight to Riposo?'

She sent him a slow smile. 'My hotel room is closer.'

His eyes twinkled in a way she'd never seen before. 'But I did not bring pyjamas or a toothbrush.'

'We can buy you a toothbrush, and you won't need pyjamas. We can go home tomorrow.'

He sobered. 'Will you be happy to live at Riposo? My family is all there and maybe you will find it too much.'

'Never,' she vowed. 'I love your family.'

He smiled. 'I do too, but I would sometimes like to have you all to myself.'

'We can always camp out in Bertha.'

'*Si*, that is perfect! Though I do not expect my family will remain at the villa for much longer. Mamma is in love, and I suspect she will soon want a place of her own. Sofia is talking about returning to Rome and taking up an internship in my company, while Maria and Giorgia say it is too much to live with their brother and want to rent a place in the town so they can go out at night and *"have more freedom".'* He frowned. 'Should I be worried?'

'No, you should not,' she told him with a laugh. 'And speaking of families, I took your advice and have spoken to both my mother and grand-father and told them of my plans. They were disappointed, but when I told them how happy this would make me, they accepted it. They even said they were happy for me.'

'But that is excellent news!'

He grinned at her and she couldn't help but grin back.

'I have more family news too,' he said. 'You will not know the name, Antonio, but you will remember the man whose life you saved.'

'The man who had a heart attack? Is he doing well?'

'He is making a good recovery, but here is the thing—he was a spy, sent by my aunt. He is her lover. They were looking for ways to undermine the restaurant.'

Her hand flew to her mouth.

'They were jealous that I had thought of creating a restaurant to honour Lorenzo. They wished they'd thought of it first. They wanted to put the restaurant out of business.'

She folded her arms. 'Which is ridiculously childish!'

'But she was so grateful that we saved her lover's life that she has given up her grudge and apologised. When I asked her, wasn't it time we were friends? she agreed.'

She leaned towards him. 'Really?'

'*Si*. It is a start.'

She pressed a hand to cheek. 'It would've made Lorenzo very happy.'

'*Si*.' His eyes darkened. 'But not as happy as you make me, Frankie. I thought I had lost you, and they were the darkest days of my life.'

'I know. This last week has been one of the worst of my life too. But now we've found one another, we won't ever lose each other again. I'll take care of your heart and you'll take care of mine.'

'This is something I solemnly vow to you.' His eyes never left hers. 'I will love you and take care of you forever.'

'Forever,' she agreed. 'And tomorrow we'll return home to Riposo.' Her home of rest. Who knew six weeks ago, all she would find there? 'And we'll work out the logistics of our future then.' The important thing was that they had a future. *Together*. 'In the meantime, Dante, I think you better kiss me again.'

He did, and then reached for her ukulele and

played 'You Are My Sunshine' with all of his love for her shining from his eyes, and without making a single mistake. Which meant she then had to kiss him again. And again.

* * * * *

Look out for the next story in the
One Summer in Italy duet
Coming soon!

And if you enjoyed this story, check out these
other great reads from Michelle Douglas

Reclusive Millionaire's Mistletoe Miracle
Wedding Date in Malaysia
Escape with Her Greek Tycoon
Cinderella and the Brooding Billionaire

All available now!